Photo by Patrick O'Hare

JANICE SHAPIRO'S stories have been published in *The North American Review*, *The Santa Monica Review*, and *The Seattle Review*. A screenwriter, she co-wrote the cult film *Dead Beat*. She is currently working on another collection of short stories and a graphic memoir, *Crushable: My Life in Crushes from Ricky Nelson to Viggo Mortensen*. She lives in Brooklyn with her husband, son, and dog.

BUMMER

and other stories

BUMMER

and other stories

JANICE SHAPIRO

Soft Skull Press

The following stories have been previously published in slightly different form: "Predation," "Tiger Beat," and "Maternity" in *The North American Review;* "Bummer," "1966," "Death and Disaster," "In Its Place," "Small," "The Old Bean," and "Ennui" in *The Santa Monica Review.*

Library of Congress Cataloging-in-Publication Data
Shapiro, Janice.
Bummer, and other stories / Janice Shapiro.
   p. cm.
ISBN-13: 978-1-59376-296-4
ISBN-10: 1-59376-296-8
1. Women—United States—Fiction. 2. United States—Social life and customs—21st century—Fiction. I. Title.
PS3619.H35597B86 2010
813'.6—dc22
                    2010010919

Cover image by Robert Longo: *Untitled (Men in the Cities), 1982*
Charcoal, graphite and ink on paper
96 x 48 inches/243.8 x 121.9 cm
Courtesy of the Artist and Metro Pictures, New York

Cover design by Domini Dragoone
Interior design by Neuwirth & Associates, Inc.
Printed in the United States of America

Soft Skull Press
An Imprint of Counterpoint LLC
1919 Fifth Street
Berkeley, CA 94710

www.softskull.com
www.counterpointpress.com

Distributed by Publishers Group West

10 9 8 7 6 5 4 3 2 1

CONTENTS

For Adam.

BUMMER
and other stories

BUMMER

M AN, I WAS HAVING a bad day. The year was 1978 and
I was twenty-one years old, in Las Vegas for the first
time because my boyfriend, Sean, had finally agreed to
marry me, but only if we made it a kind of *Fear and Loathing*–
themed event, which basically meant we had to drive a rented
Cadillac Eldorado convertible across the desert with Sean in
the backseat, staring up at the sky and taking like a ridiculous
amount of drugs while I couldn't take any because of the baby.
Or whatever you call that thing growing inside of you.

Well, as I'm sure you can guess, the wedding didn't exactly
go off as planned. Meaning, there was no wedding. Meaning,
high on mescaline and acid and speed and pot and who knows
what, Sean claimed to have some kind of a vision of a burning
teepee in the middle of the MGM Grand's swimming pool
and declared it a sign of the dire things to come if we became

man and wife. I wasn't buying, and it wasn't just because I believed getting married was the-right-thing-to-do-when-you're-pregnant. I wanted to marry Sean because I loved him. Isn't that dumb? Dumb, but true. But you know how there are people in this world who are incredibly good at getting what they want (my sister being one of them, big time)? Like they just have a talent or skill, or good fortune, or I don't know what, but whatever it is, I *don't* have any of it. I mean, I *never* get what I want and that day was no exception.

"Fine, you fuckhead," I screamed when we were stopped at a red light on that hideous street where there's like one huge hotel lined up after another but which still manages to feel completely empty and bare. "I wouldn't marry you if you were the last hard dick in the universe!"

Sean shrugged and opened his car door and that was when I kicked him, and Sean kind of fell out of the car. I immediately sped away and the last I saw of Sean was the top of his rainbow-colored Mohawk before it was obscured by a swarm of black fezzes as a large contingent of vacationing Shriners merrily crossed the street.

In 1978 they didn't have such strict rules about what's good and not good for you when you're pregnant and so having like one margarita didn't seem like such a heinous crime. I mean, I wasn't even that far along. Maybe six weeks or something, but it being Las Vegas where in my mind everything was just plain crummy, it was a crummy margarita, tasting mainly like soap, and I was angrily not enjoying it at the bar adjacent to the Sands swimming pool when this guy, the kind you would just think would be in a place like Las Vegas, no stranger to either polyester or Old Spice, sat down right next to me and then proceeded to stare.

Now, I have to admit, I was used to being looked at, not just because I did happen to be kind of pretty at the time, but also I was what you might call an early adopter of the punk style. I mean, even in L.A. at that time there weren't that many people with lime green hair and safety pins through their lips. That is how Sean and I met—at a Screamers show at the Masque where I was immediately taken with his luminescent skin, thick Irish accent, and multi-multi-multi-pierced eyebrow. But at that moment, that day in Vegas, I was totally *not* in the mood to be the freak sideshow attraction, so I just glared back at the guy and said, "Would you mind?"

"Excuse me?" he said, his voice kind of awkward and strange with some sort of foreign accent.

"Could you please get your fucking face out of mine?"

The guy looked confused for a second before he smiled one of those smiles that no matter how much you weren't in the mood could almost win you over.

"Perfect," he laughed and that was when I heard the tang of Latin America in his *r*'s. Now, I know there are people who welcome the opportunity to engage in conversations with foreigners, the chance to expand one's horizons, broaden your point of view, and all that shit, but the total fact is I am not one of those people—unless the foreign country in question happens to be, say, Ireland, which I could tell right away was *not* where this guy hailed from.

"Fuck you," I sneered, and grabbed my drink and carried it inside the hotel, which as soon as the glass door closed behind me I knew was not where I wanted to be. For one thing, the air was practically toxic from all the fucking cigarette smoke and the gallons of spilled drinks and the sickening stench of all that crummily prepared food festering just beneath the strange, claustrophobic, permanent-twilight lighting that tries to hold out the utterly false promise of an endless, perfect night. And then there was also the noise—the rhythmless clangings and repetitive jingles and occasional cries of greed and disappointment, and since I was someone who never had the chance to grow accustomed to the concept of winning, unlike my sister who always just assumed being a winner was her goddamned birthright, the gaming tables held no allure for me. But I was still holding that drink I'd paid way too much for and had nothing but a long, lonely drive back home across a remarkably unscenic desert ahead of me, so I took a seat in an abandoned lounge area, right in front of an empty stage that was set up for a most likely too-eager-to-please, top-notch combo that, if they had been playing, would've certainly made me puke.

How the fuck could Sean do this to me? I stared up at the empty stage and asked no one but myself and was just about to plunge headfirst into a long, purifying cry when a shiny penny suddenly landed on the small black cocktail table.

"A . . . er . . . *penny* for your thoughts."

There he was again—that guy, smiling down at me in all of his polyester and Old Spice glory. I decided he was probably in his midthirties and the type who would do the rhumba naked in front of the bathroom mirror each morning, and one of the reasons I didn't like to associate with nonnative-English speakers was there just seemed to be too much room for misunderstanding, plus a lot people from other countries have really odd senses of humor and it just makes me really nervous to be around people who laugh at things you just *know* are not funny.

"You're corny," I said, unpleasantly. "You are a fucking cornball."

The guy smiled as if I had complimented him on his hairstyle and then took the seat next to me.

"So . . ." he said, but before he could say anything more, I held up my hand, stopping him.

"Look at me," I demanded, speaking slowly and deliberately. "I am the total opposite of corn. Get it? I probably hate everything you love . . . like kitties and Christmas and Mom. I love everything you hate like blood and despair and dirty, used-up toothpicks. You and me? We have nothing in common! *Comprende? Nada!* So will you please leave me the fuck alone?"

"Yes . . . well . . . I was wondering," the guy continued as if I had just made some kind of polite generic comment on the weather. "Could I please buy you something to eat?"

"I'm not hungry!" I screamed. "I hate food!"

His smile brightened and then he started to laugh as if I had just said the wittiest thing in the world.

"Perfect," he said, and then he did something I really wish he hadn't. He reached out and ran one of his hands slowly down my spine. That was it. A hand moving down my back. But if there's one thing I'm a sucker for, it's a certain kind of touch, you know, the kind that's done just the right way, so it renders you suddenly unable to move or speak, like a victim of a goddamned stun-gun blast—totally overwhelmed with a desire for more.

It was very unlike me to sleep with a guy I just met. I mean, I knew Sean for a couple of weeks before I slept with him, and when I was in art school, I'd go celibate for months, not for want of opportunities, I just happen to be picky about that kind of thing, and I didn't know if I was doing what I was doing out of something like anger or hopelessness or just a desire to step firmly into that forever, big, bright future—but whatever the reason, there I was, up in this foreign guy's rather fabulous suite somewhere in the Sands Hotel, rolling around the king-size bed.

Man, he was good too. There was nothing corny or polyester about the stranger in bed. He just had that natural ability, that heightened sensitivity and excellent sense of timing that makes a person a great tennis partner or fuck. I mean, it really was one of those "thoroughly delightful experiences," as my sister would put it, that for the time it lasted took my mind off my problems and tentatively lifted me out of my funk, with one exception—my breasts, which were larger and more sensitive than usual since the pregnancy, slightly throbbed the whole time with a strange, dull pain.

"I just had a good . . . how do you call it? *Feeling* about you," the guy said, running his fingers lazily through the spikes in my hair as we lay there, side by side, catching our breaths.

"Yeah? Why?" I asked, and he shrugged in a foreign, accented way.

"I don't know," he said. "You looked like a . . . a . . . a *winner*."

"Ha," I said. The way he had said *winner*, it sounded more like *wiener*, but I knew what he meant, and now that the sex part of the deal was over I just wanted to get out of there. "Mind if I use your shower?"

"Be my guest," he said, and leaned against the pillows to watch me get out of the bed, silently admiring my body which even I knew was extremely beautiful.

"By the way, man," I said, tenderly cupping my full and still slightly hurting breasts. "I'm pregnant."

"That's nice," he said, smiling in that same pleasant way, and at that moment he looked so much like one of those all-suave Latin-lover playboys in a corny '60s movie that I expected a jazzy Nelson Riddle instrumental to start to play while he coolly lit two cigarettes and held one out to me, but that didn't happen. He just reached over to the bedside table and picked up a *Guide to Las Vegas* and began to move his lips silently, his brow wrinkling in concentration before he started to laugh at something I would bet you anything was *not* funny.

IT WAS in the shower that I started to worry about the future again—something I had always been loath to do. See, the main reason I decided to study painting in the first place was because it allows a person to exist primarily in the moment, you know, experience each brush stroke as it comes, the end of a piece presenting itself when it chooses. But this being-fucking-pregnant business just changed everything, man. I mean, suddenly, I had to think about what was really going to happen to me and the baby. Like, *what?*

When I thought Sean might marry me, I could get into the idea of actually raising a kid, maybe even in Ireland where it would grow up speaking English but with that great accent, and in a culture that still had something to fuel the fire of deep-felt-to-die-for beliefs. But when I took Sean out of the picture and it was just me and the kid living together in my small apartment in the Miracle Mile, doing stuff like eating a lot of Kraft macaroni and cheese and reading and reread-ing my ancient collection of *Tintins*, surrounded by paintings that seemed to grow more trite with each passing day, being a mother just didn't seem all that appealing.

But what to do? What to do? The firm beat of the shower pounded pleasantly against my shoulders and I watched, mes-merized, the endless beads of water slowly inching their way over my now nicely rounded breasts, and I couldn't help but wonder where Sean was at that moment and if (considering the amount of drugs he had coursing through his veins) he was all right. But that was another thing about Las Vegas I was hating. It was like its own tacky galaxy and even if Sean was somewhere near, everything was so big and spread out in such a purposefully disorienting way, he might as well have been on an entirely different planet.

"*Ay caramba*," I sighed and wanted to cry but that was when I noticed the small white plastic bottle of medicated sham-poo. I picked it up and squinted at the label. The medication had some long name I wasn't familiar with and couldn't even begin to pronounce and the patient it had been prescribed for was Jose Something-or-other. The last name was com-pletely washed out. Curious, I unscrewed the cap and poured a small drop onto my hand and gasped because the pale blue gel burned like hell. Immediately I washed it off and then just stared suspiciously at the bottle, wondering what the fuck did this Jose guy have that needed to be treated with shit like that,

and began to fervently hope it wasn't anything too contagious, and that's when I had that hideous feeling you get when
you've just slept with someone you know absolutely nothing
about, like every cell of your being is suddenly forced to band
together around the one hope that luck won't betray you too
badly this time, that the repercussions from this particularly
foolish leap from a moderate sense of self-control into the
erotic pool of who-knows-what won't prove to be too bad or
wide sweeping.

I got out of the shower and wrapped myself in a large white
towel and carried the bottle of medicated shampoo into the
bedroom and was about to ask the guy what exactly was this
shit used for, when I saw the bed was now empty. Looking
around, I noticed my red vinyl mini bridal dress was still lying
in a crumpled heap on the golden shag carpet, but the guy's
100 percent polyester ensemble was gone. A faint whiff of
freshly applied Old Spice hung around the room and when I
sat down on the bed to regroup my thoughts and figure out
my next plan of action, I noticed the hastily written note lying
on top of one of the pillows. It said:

"*Adios mi querida. Muchas gracias para todo. Su amigo, Ramon.*"

"'Your *friend*, Ramon?'" I rolled my eyes and shook my head,
writing off this delusional interpretation of our relationship as
a clear example of the gap between our respective cultures.
Then I looked at the name on the bottle of shampoo again. It
was indeed Jose and I wondered if it might actually belong
to someone else, not the guy I had just slept with, but even I
wasn't buying it and that was when I decided the best course
of action would be to take the bottle of shampoo with me,
drive home as quickly as I could, and show it to my sister's

husband, who just happened to be a big shot MD. Marcus, I reassured myself, would be able to tell me exactly what kind of disease this guy had and if exposure to it posed any kind of health threat to the born or unborn alike.

"He's a loser."

"So what? I'm a loser too."

"No you're not, Alison! Will you stop talking like that? You are not a loser. You are a very talented artist who hasn't had the right breaks yet, but you're still very young, and with perseverance and determination you *will* eventually succeed."

FYI, that was the conversation my sister Jules and I had after I brought Sean to her house for dinner. I don't even know why I did it. I think it must've been her idea. Ever since our mom died when I was ten and Jules twenty, she has felt this annoying sense of responsibility for me, so, of course, when she heard I had a new boyfriend, she had to check him out, right?

The dinner hadn't been a barrel of laughs. What with Sean having consumed beforehand like six pints at the pub in Laurel Canyon where he worked, and my brother-in-law Marcus being all preoccupied about some malpractice lawsuit, and my sister looking all tense, but still way too smiley, because even though she always got everything she wanted, the one thing she wanted more than anything else in the world (meaning a kid) was for some still-unknown physiological reason being denied her, and me just being my absolute worst, as I always was around my sister, basically the meal was just something to endure.

"So, how do you like living in our country?" Jules queried Sean, serving him an unasked-for second helping of salmon in what I took to be an aggressive manner.

"It's okay," Sean said, and raised his eyebrows so that all of the safety pins clanged together as he looked hopefully at his almost-empty wine glass.

I saw Jules's eyes briefly meet Marcus's before she asked, "Oh? And what's so *okay* about it?"

"Dunno," Sean said, and quickly finished the so-deeply-red-it's-almost-brown liquid left in his glass. "Maybe it's the sky, you know."

"The sky," Jules repeated, flatly, and if we weren't sitting in her house, eating her food and drinking her expensive wine, I would've jumped up and smacked her in the nose.

"It's different from what we have back home," Sean said in that earnest way he said things when he was drunk. "There's just like . . . like . . . more of it here, isn't there?"

I nodded my head eagerly. I knew this wasn't going over big, but I also didn't care.

"Yeah," I said. "Could someone pass the vino down?"

"Marcus," my sister turned to her husband, who wisely refused to relinquish the whole bottle over to me and Sean and so instead carefully refilled our glasses before returning the bottle to its place within his reach alone. "Is it really possible for there to be more sky in one part of the world than another?"

"Who knows?" Marcus said in that dismissive way that doctors speak if you ask them something that might make them feel like for one second they don't know everything.

"Always an excellent answer," Jules said, unable to hide her irritability any longer as she stabbed a green bean and glared at the safety pin in my lip. "*Who* knows?"

Basically the whole evening meant nothing to Sean, but

afterward I decided never to speak to my sister again, so when she called the next day to convince me I was too good for Sean, I said, "Save the pep talk, Jules. I'm a loser and I like it."

Then I hung up and got back into bed where Sean was snoring softly. His sickly white skin looked even whiter and even more sickly on my hand-me-down, soft, pink peach cotton sheets. A comforting, cool, dry body heat pressed against me as I wrapped my arms around his narrow torso, and his morning breath smelled slightly of rusting steel and, you know, it was true: At that moment in time, I did like being a loser because if punk was about anything other than fashion to begin with, it was about the glorification of the losers of the world; it gave us a voice, it gave us a look, it gave us a kind of cockeyed dignity that practically felt like inspiration. And with that hotheaded pride pumping hard out of my heart like a Scotty Asheton drum beat from an early Stooges song, I roused Sean with my kisses and touch, pulling him into a current of proud rebellion, making love for the first and only time with my diaphragm not where I knew it really should've been.

BUT I digress.

So, I was in the middle of the Sands parking lot, in the middle of the day, with the sun smacking me hard, trying to remember where I left the rented Cadillac, anxious to be back on the road so I could reach my sister's oh-so-contemporary pad in the hills of beautiful Encino before it was too late to ask Marcus about the shampoo, when I opened my purse and felt it: an unfamiliar round and plastic object with a smooth center and rough edges. Slowly, I pulled it out of the dark cave of my purse and stopped in my tracks when I saw that it was a hideous green Sands hotel gambling chip worth $100.

"Oh my God! That fucking freak!" I screamed, realizing that the foreign guy must have slipped the chip into my purse when I was in the shower. *"How the fuck dare he? I was fucking using him just as much as he was using me!"*

A horn honked loudly and I looked up to see a Lincoln Town Car, its headlights perversely on in the bright desert sun, and man, if you were to pick the absolute most wrong moment to honk at me, this would have to be it. So I reeled around and gave the driver the finger and screamed, "HEL-TER SKELTER, YOU FUCKING PIG! SUCK ON THIS!"

Then I threw the $100 chip right at its tinted windshield.

Now, don't even ask me how what happened next happened because I can't tell you. But somehow, the chip hit the Town Car in a probably one-in-a-million way that made it fly backward and land smack-dab right inside my open purse again.

The Lincoln swerved around me and its harsh exhaust filled my nostrils and the echo of its angry horn rang in my ears. I could feel the stirred-up parking lot dust settling on my sweat-coated skin but I just stood there, glaring at the chip resting once again inside my faux-leopard-skin pocket book among the rented Cadillac's keys; Chinese change purse; a few spare safety pins, sterilized; and the stolen bottle of medicated shampoo. I kept standing there, staring at the chip, surrounded by like five million shiny cars emptily soaking up that cruel desert heat that comes on so strong and then vanishes so quickly into that equally harsh night chill and all I could do was shake my head and mutter, "Bummer."

MAN, I was hating Vegas. I mean, the doors that I used to go back into the Sands suddenly didn't seem like the same doors I had just exited through, and the elevators looked all wrong even though I was pretty sure they were the ones that carried me down from the guy's room, which I all at once realized I couldn't even remember the number of.

That was when I decided to ask for a little assistance.

The man behind the reception desk of the Sands Hotel just looked at me. Now, I admit I didn't have a lot to work with— the two possible first names, either Jose or Ramon—and yeah, it was a big hotel with thousands of rooms occupied by thousands of guests, but I honestly believed that with the right kind of old-fashioned American know-how, that can-do spirit glorified in like a million Frank Capra movies, he (meaning the guy at the reception desk) and I could have figured out the foreign guy's room number, thus allowing me to give back that damned, fucking-to-hell chip.

"I'm sorry," I said as nicely as I could, which wasn't easy because usually when I talked to anyone in a suit, rudeness came leaking out of me like pee. "I don't know this guy's last name. But can't you check and see if you have any Joses or Ramons registered?"

The man looked at me for a few more seconds before his gaze traveled up to the gaudy chandelier that seemed to be hanging rather ominously over my head and said, "No."

The fucking fascist.

WELL, THERE I was inside the fucking Sands Hotel with this $100 chip in my purse and the faint odor of Old Spice clinging unpleasantly to my clothes, anxious just to get the hell out of

Vegas but unwilling to leave until I straightened up this little misunderstanding and made sure Jose or Ramon or whatever his name was wouldn't live out the rest of his life thinking I was just some Vegas whore, because, as petty as it sounds, at that point in time, I couldn't live with that.

So maybe the best way to picture this next part of the story is to imagine you're looking into a kaleidoscope and in some of those fractured pieces of colorful glass there's me, right? Alison. Did I tell you my name, yet? Well, it's Alison. So, there's good old Alison wandering all over the whole stinking place with that sickening feeling you get when you have no idea where you are and no hope of ever figuring it out. See? There's Alison wandering past aisles and aisles of gaudy slot machines, and there she is in the Gala Buffet Restaurant, and there, zigzagging through a maze of lounge chairs in the pool area, all the while looking for Jose or Ramon or whatever his name was, but it being Alison, it would be a pretty safe bet Alison wouldn't find what Alison was looking for, and the fact is, I didn't.

And I was getting tired too. That was another thing that happened when I was pregnant. I'd get tired really quickly. Like one or two slam dances and I was off the floor for the night, and after my unsuccessful, exhaustive search of the Sands, I found myself back in the casino and all at once I didn't give a fuck what that guy thought of me. He, I finally realized, was an empty station my train had made a short stop in, practically meaningless except for the nagging worry about disease, but it was 1978 and we still believed there was a cure for everything, so I wasn't even that worried about *that*, and really, more than anything at that moment I just wanted to sit down and the first chair my weary eyes rested on was at an empty blackjack table, and that's when it hit me. Why not just do something I was good at for a change? I mean, why not use my not-inconsiderable ability to lose to rid myself of that hideous green chip forever.

So I sat down at the blackjack table but I didn't get too comfortable because I knew it was going to be a very short rest. I mean, how long does it take to lose a hand of cards? But I milked it for all it was worth, taking a long time to pull the chip out of my purse and then just looking at it in a considering way, never acknowledging the dealer, a kind of scary-looking chick with frizzed-up black hair and too much foundation makeup, who just stood there distractedly shuffling and reshuffling the cards.

Finally, she placed the deck on the table but still kept her hand on it, and I saw her fingernails were painted the same overly gardened green as the chip.

"You want me break it?" she asked in a totally bored voice.

"What?" I said.

"Break it," she said, and impatiently motioned with one of her green-tipped fingers at the $100 chip.

That was when I noticed what totally cool, catlike eyes she had. They were this perfect color of brown and yellow and black all weirdly spun together and were so beautiful I could suddenly imagine men from all over this big country coming to Vegas and falling hard for this dealer, blindly handing over chip after chip, and they wouldn't even know it was because of the eyes. That color. Those sexy cat eyes that always seemed to be looking for trouble even when they weren't.

And all at once, I was glad I was going to lose that $100 to her, feeling for probably the first time in a million years actually happy and light and easy about everything. I smiled and carefully laid the chip on the table and said, "Twenty-one's my age, so it might as well be my game."

The dealer hardly moved, just squinted those fabulous eyes and mumbled in this wonderfully unconvincing way, "Might as well."

And then she dealt the cards so fast it almost took my breath away and for a few seconds I didn't realize what I had lying before me which, of course, was a ten of clubs and an ace of diamonds.

"Hey, isn't that . . . ?" I started to say, but before I could finish my sentence, with a really quite elegant sweeping motion, my cards were gone, but the $100 chip stayed and beside it now rested an identical $100 chip plus a queasy pinkish-colored $50.

I looked up and my eyes met the stone-still dealer's, and I was pleased to see there was nothing different in her beautiful eyes, no shame of loss or admiration for my good fortune, just that catch-me-go-to-hell look of hers.

Since we were the only two at the table I wasn't too embarrassed to ask, "So, like, what do I do now, man?"

"Whatever you want, man," she answered, and really seemed like she couldn't care less and I was loving her even more because she was just so, well, *cool*.

"I'm pregnant," I found myself saying even though I knew it had nothing to do with anything. "And my boyfriend who's Irish won't marry me and I just slept with this total stranger who probably knows about ten words of English and has some kind of weird scalp disease that I'm just hoping isn't contagious, if you know what I mean."

Her eyes flickered in such a way that made me think she knew exactly what I meant, but all she said was: "So . . . are you in or out?"

I thought about this for a second and then just nodded.

"How much?" the dealer asked, and her green-nailed finger began to tap impatiently on the deck again.

I looked down at the three chips on the table before me and shrugged.

"All the way," I said.

WELL, I suppose you can guess what happened next, which was once again, the cat-eyed dealer dealt and this time there was an ace of spades and queen of diamonds staring up at me and more chips were quickly pushed across the table.

I, of course, let that bet ride and this time I got the jack of clubs and ace of hearts. Then there was one more hand of twenty-one or blackjack or whatever you call it, but whatever it was, it was the weirdest fucking thing in the world. I couldn't lose for the life of me. I mean, I didn't get any more blackjacks, but still, I just kept winning and winning and winning and it was the strangest feeling because with each win it was like someone had placed another brick on my shoulders, until I felt so weighted down with like an entire stadium of good fortune I didn't know how I would ever move again, and for the first time I felt sorry for my sister. I mean, the responsibility of having good luck, I suddenly realized, was a very heavy thing.

I was something like a few thousand dollars ahead and I had stopped looking at the cards or the chips because when I did, I would get that vertigo feeling and I was afraid I might pass out, so I watched the dealer who acted as if me just winning and winning off her meant nothing and would probably still be acting like that if her boss hadn't come up and, with a light tap on her shoulder, silently sent her packing.

The dealer took this with that same admirable indifference with which she faced life and, without saying good-bye, placed the deck neatly onto the table and turned to leave.

"Wait," I said and dug around under the mountain of chips and found what I hoped to be the original $100.

"Good luck, man," I said, and carefully transferred the chip into her hand.

"Thanks, man," she said, flatly.

The new dealer was someone I had no desire to get into anything with—he was just one of those guys that came out of the same mold as the unhelpful guy behind the reception desk, a nerd, a total loser, but a loser who had no pride, so I scooped up my chips, dumped them into my faux-leopard-skin purse and walked away.

I THINK I was passing that same little stage I was sitting in front of before, but now there was this hideous band performing, and as if to insult me personally they were playing a horrible version of one of my favorite songs, Elvis Costello's "Alison" (my name, right?), and the lead singer, this lady dressed in all shiny shit, was milking the line "My aim is true" for all it was worth.

A shudder of revulsion swept through my body and I was

about to start screaming for them to stop! Have some mercy and stop playing that song! Sing something else! A fucking Beatles or Elton John! But then I noticed the colors of a synthetic rainbow fanned out across one of the black cocktail tables.

I walked over and saw Sean was asleep, his head partly on the table and partly off, his mouth open and a tiny pool of drool puddling around his cheeks. And I thought how I could lose a lot of things, but hearing Sean sing the Irish songs he sang only when he was too drunk and homesick to realize how corny they were, or feeling his hands shoving me against the stage at another Clash concert, or seeing his cockeyed smile when he looked at my paintings but never spoke of them ever, like they were just too sacred or something to talk about, were all things I just couldn't face losing.

So I slowly knelt until my head was as high as the table and whispered, "Hey."

His eyes opened, and from out of the altered world in which I could tell he was still traveling, he must've seen me because he smiled in that sweet, fermented way of his that always reminded me of stepped-upon grapes, and he said, "Alison."

"Guess what?" I said. "I'm rich."

"Cool," he said.

"Yeah," I said and then took a deep breath before saying what I said next which was, "So, like now do you think you might want to marry me?"

Sean blinked and pressed his lips together and then said the word I suddenly knew I wanted to hear, the one thing he could say that would put everything right again in the small stubborn world that I used to call all my own, but knew it was not, nor no longer ever would be again.

"No," he said. "Uh-uh."

And I couldn't help from smiling, my heart overflowing with so much love and gratitude I could practically feel it spilling through my body and going straight into the baby's still-forming heart as I said, "Cool."

1966

I T WAS THE SUMMER of the dead nurses and that sniper in
Texas and we were not allowed to walk on my grandparents'
lawn because of the frogs. I was nine years old, growing up in
the San Fernando Valley, a place not unlike my grandparents'
yard, homelands for populations that had for various reasons
exploded. In the Valley's case, it was with millions of children,
the famous baby boom generation; and in my grandparents'
yard, billions of tiny amphibians, refugees of that concrete
eyesore known as the Los Angeles River.

Our neighborhood in North Hollywood was flat and heavy
with trees. In the summer the air got dry and hot and dirty,
and everywhere—in the leaves, on the driveways, and in our
hair—was the faint smell of chlorine from all of our neighbors' pools. We didn't have a pool. It was one of those things
my sister Evelyn and I would occasionally beg our father for,

but he always said the same thing: "We don't need a pool. We have the Houstons."

The Houstons were our next-door neighbors and extremely generous with their swimming pool. We could use it whenever we wanted. Still, it wasn't the same as having our own. We knew this. Our parents knew this. The difference was we cared, my sister and I. Our parents didn't. But then one night that summer, the summer of 1966, when our father seemed to be in a particularly bad mood, quieter and less connected than usual, we asked if we could please, please, *please* put a swimming pool in our backyard and he stunned us by saying, "We'll see."

My mother shot him a look across the dinner table. My father saw it. Evelyn and I saw it. It was a look that clearly asked, "What is the meaning of this?"

We held our breath, waiting to see if our father was going to take back his words, but he went back to eating his short rib and staring out the window at our empty driveway. Our father had said, "We'll see," and "We'll see" was how it stood.

Evelyn and I were joyous. We skipped around the house. We threw our arms around each other like conquering heroes. We kicked our legs out and sang the cancan. Our father had said, "We'll see."

"That doesn't mean yes," our teenage babysitter, Bobbi, told us. She was taking care of us on a Saturday night and had her hair up in curlers, but her lips glowed beneath a sheen of frosted pink lipstick and her eyes were surrounded by expertly painted black lines that continued out toward her temples in a Liz-as-Cleopatra look. Bobbi had brought over her denim-covered notebook because she was supposed to do homework after Evelyn and I went to sleep. She was going to summer school because she had failed English, math, and Spanish in the tenth grade, and Bobbi was depressed about going to summer school. She was depressed to be taking care of us on a Saturday night, instead of being out on a date. She was depressed because her parents hated her, something Evelyn and I knew because Bobbi lived next door, in the house on the other side than the Houstons, and if we crouched down beside the window in our parents' bedroom we could listen to her fights with her parents.

"You hate me!" Bobbi would scream and then we never heard either of her parents say one word to dispute this.

Bobbi was pretty, if a little overweight. When her brown hair wasn't in curlers, she teased it high and was really good at putting on makeup so that she looked grown-up but not grown-up like our mother, but grown-up like a lady in a car commercial, one that drives a totally impractical convertible too fast around dangerous canyon curves. When she babysat for us, Bobbi spent a lot of time talking to different boys on the phone and Evelyn and I would sit close, silently listening as her voice got sweet and girlish, her laugh easy and fleeting. Basically, Bobbi held us in contempt. We were not what she wanted to do, ever, but she was a teenager. She was pretty. We loved her. Evelyn and I. We loved Bobbi with a purity I don't think we loved anyone else with.

"You got a D on your Spanish test," I said, nosily flipping through the pages of her notebook, worried because I knew Bobbi's bad grades were the basis of a lot of terrible fights and I hated it when Bobbi's parents yelled at her.

She grabbed the notebook away from me. "You know, when

I was your age I got straight As, too." Bobbi told me this not like a warning, but a fact, a premonition of things that were to come that I would not believe would come at the time and then I would be wrong.

TIME IN the summer moved in that bloated way forward. Occasionally, our mother took us to Muscle Beach for the day or to visit our grandparents who lived near Griffith Park in an area called Atwater just off of the Golden State Freeway. But for the most part we stayed in the Valley, surrounded by the low mountains that seemed to hold us captive along with the dirty air and the heat.

That summer Evelyn had her passion and I had mine. At age ten and a half, my sister became an obsessive Dodgers fan. She memorized the lineup, knew all the players' batting averages, the team's exact daily standing in the National League. She was a thin, dark girl and had such a wondrous smile even a mouthful of braces could not dull its charm. To the outside world, she was sweet and shy, but I knew her true personality to be spiteful, manipulative, and mean. What my sister was beyond else was a killjoy. If anyone (especially me) was having a good time, she was masterful at finding ways to destroy it, but that summer, making me miserable wasn't really her top priority. Instead she preferred to lie on her bed and listen to the Dodgers game on our transistor radio, cheering and moaning, strange solitary sounds that should have been lost in a crowd, but weren't.

My passion was also a lonely one. No one I knew was as obsessed with the murders as me. I read and reread every article in the *L.A. Times*, first about the poor nurses killed in

Chicago and then a couple of weeks later about the gunman in the tower at the University of Texas. I sat at my parents' desk and studied the photos in *LIFE* magazine of the sniper's attack in Austin, memorizing the exact position the coed affected beside the fountain in order to dodge the sniper's bullets, and laid under a tree in our front yard, imagining what it would've been like to be the lone surviving nurse balanced on the ledge of the second-story window, calling out at dawn, "Help me! Help me! Help me! Everybody is dead! I'm the only one alive on the sampan!"

MY MOTHER looked terrible in bathing suits. Her legs, horribly knock-kneed, were all lumpy and riddled with varicose veins. She was small breasted, and the points of her padded bathing suit sagged slightly, and despite the suffocating, girdlelike material that struggled to hold her in, give the appearance of tautness, the illusion of control, her abdomen protruded stubbornly. My mother, at age thirty-three, would plan another diet, vow to eat more Knudsen cottage cheese, forsake sugar for saccharine, tune in to Jack LaLanne more religiously, and then, knowing she looked terrible, would throw on a short shift and bravely escort me and my sister out the back door, down the driveway, onto the street where anyone could see her, and then quickly up the Houstons' driveway, where we would pass through the gate hung with the sign, WE DON'T SWIM IN YOUR TOILET, PLEASE DON'T PEE IN OUR POOL.

My mother didn't know how to swim. What she would do was kind of glide from the shallow to deep end, keeping her head so high the bottom of her bubble 'do never touched water. Evelyn and I took lessons. We knew how to swim, at least better than our mother, but that summer I too swam mostly with my head above the water. I did this because I was secretly on watch, scanning the rooftops of the homes around us, looking for snipers, afraid to go under, afraid that once I gave up the vigil, once I let go of my fears and allowed myself to enjoy the cool, calm quiet below the pool's surface, I was risking becoming yet another direct hit.

MY FATHER started to bring home brochures from pool companies, and after dinner Evelyn and I would crowd around his chair and look at the beautiful color pictures of sparkling swimming pools, admiring the different shapes, rectangular, oblong, and the ever-popular kidney. The one I wanted had a kind of free form shape with fake sparkly lavalike rocks and a waterfall. We both wanted a diving board. We both wanted a slide. My father wouldn't let us touch the brochures. He held them just out of our reach and then carefully refolded them before putting them away in a special pocket in his briefcase.

"Do you think we're really going to get a swimming pool?" Evelyn and I would ask our mother during the day when our dad was at work and she was ours, something that she wasn't quite when my father was around.

"I don't know," she'd answer, and shrug her shoulders and then keep them around her ears for a really long time to emphasize her uncertainty. *I don't know* was not the answer we wanted, so we kept asking, at least once a day, trying to get a little hope from our mother, something she has never given out with much liberality.

Because of her bad grades, Bobbi was being kept on a short leash that summer and she was forced to hang around her house a lot. When her mother was out she sat on her back porch and smoked cigarettes and Evelyn and I would go over and sit with her, happily breathing in the sour smoke that she exhaled with admirable expertise for a fifteen-year-old girl.

"You're not getting a swimming pool," she said sullenly after we had finished telling her all about the pictures in the brochures, describing the intricate curves in our favorite slide and drawing with a stick in the dirt the leading shape of the swimming pool of the moment.

"But Dad said we are," we told her, stretching the truth a little.

Bobbi shook her head and looked over to the fence that separated her yard from the Smalls'. The Smalls had a teen-age son, Freddy, who spent a lot of time lying underneath his car. Freddy was one of the boys Bobbi talked to on the phone when she babysat for us. We asked her once if she loved him and she laughed and called him a geek, but still, her voice got sweet when she talked to him, just like when she talked to every other boy.

"Your father is messing with your heads," she told us, and took the last drag on her cigarette, exhaling a thick plume of smoke into our waiting faces.

We didn't like to contradict Bobbi. We knew she didn't like us and we didn't want to do or say anything that would make her dislike us more. So we watched silently as she stamped out her cigarette with the heel of her flip-flop, picked up the butt, and tossed it over the fence and into the Smalls' backyard.

"Hey, Bobbi," I said, trying to stall her for just a few more seconds before she disappeared inside her house.

"What?" She looked at me, impatiently.

"Um," I said, trying to think up something interesting to say, something that might even endear me to her a little bit.

"Are they saying, *Hang on, stupid* in that song or *Hang on, Snoopy?*"

Bobbi sighed and without a word, walked inside, shaking her head at what truly pathetic creatures Evelyn and I were. The back door slammed shut, leaving us sitting on the Edelsteins' back steps for a few minutes before we realized what a weird place it was for us to be and that Bobbi's mother could drive up at any second and then we would have to say hello to her, something we hated to do because, basically, all grown-ups scared us to death.

WHAT I found somewhat heartening was the fact that the one surviving nurse escaped being murdered by hiding under the bed. That had always been my plan when the murderer came to our house to kill our family and I was pleased to learn it was proven to be a successful one. But I knew it was all a matter of timing. I had to get under the bed before the murderer saw me and so I had to hear him when he first entered our house. I had to always be listening for his heavy murderer footsteps walking around the kitchen, through the service porch, past the furnace, and toward my sister's and my bedroom. Needless to say, I did not sleep very well.

"Why would someone do it?" I asked my mother, and she shook her head and answered, "There are crazy people out there."

This answer gave me no comfort. Crazy was a wild card. Crazy was random. Crazy was bad luck. The poor couple looking at engagement rings in the jeweler's window when they were struck down by the sniper's fire in Austin: bad luck. The three nurses who returned home from their dates while the murderer was still in their house: bad luck. Bad luck—it could happen to anyone. It could happen to me. And there was no escaping that.

AFTER DINNER, my father got out the tape measure and Evelyn and I followed him outside to the backyard where we all walked around, trying to figure out the best place for the swimming pool. Evelyn and I worked the tape measure and my father jotted down figures on a pad of paper, but mostly he just silently stared off into space.

At thirty-five, our father was not bad looking. He had a head of nice thick, dark hair. He wore horn-rimmed glasses and had an appealing overbite. When I was a little younger I thought he was the handsomest man in the world, and I remember one day when my mother brought us to visit him at work and he came out to the vast marble hall to greet us I was surprised other people were not swooning at the sight of him. But gradually I think I attained a more realistic assessment of my father's looks. I understood that he was not bad looking. That was what my father was.

That and moody. The mood he most often was in was distant. He talked to our mother, but rarely to us. I cannot remember my father ever asking me about my day at school. I cannot remember my father reading me a single book. I cannot remember my father ever starting a bath. What he did when he came home from work was keep to himself unless he was called upon by our mother to be the disciplinarian and then he took on that role with a frightening amount of zeal.

"When are we going to get the swimming pool?" Evelyn and I asked him every night, hoping to hear, *Tomorrow. Tomorrow will be the day your dreams all come true, my sweet, lovely, adorable little daughters!* But my dad never said that. When asked when we were going to get the pool, he always shook his head and was quiet for a while before finally saying, "I don't know."

My mother did not join us outside in the backyard. She did the dishes and then called us in, one by one, for our baths. While we were bathing, she ironed and typed business letters for my dad. She knew the pool was never going to happen. She knew we could never afford one, that we were just barely holding onto our middle-class existence as it was. She would not join my father in giving us false hope for something that we wanted so much but that we would never have. And yet she never stopped him either.

I see now that my father did this with not the kindest of intents. At best, his feelings about my sister and me were conflicted. He took very little pleasure in being a parent. Mostly, I think, he resented us. He resented us for being girls. He resented us for taking my mother's attention away from him. He resented having to be the breadwinner, going to a job he didn't like, managing the grand old Subway Terminal Building in downtown L.A., which was owned by his rich cousin, Wally. If and when a murderer came to our house, I somehow knew my father could not be counted upon to protect us, that my sole shot at survival was to give the appearance of never having existed at all.

BOBBI WAS not doing well in summer school. She was given even more restrictions, basically put under house arrest. She was miserable and could not hide it. She stopped smoking cigarettes and just sat on the back steps and cried.

Our mothers spoke in hushed voices through the hedges that separated our front lawns. There was talk of a private girls' school, of refusing to allow Bobbi to get her learner's permit, of sending her to live with her grandparents in Kentucky.

"The problem is she's boy-crazy," Mrs. Edelstein would say to my mother, who listened with true sympathy and dread of things to come.

"What do you want?" we'd ask Bobbi, sitting beside her as she wept, secretly admiring the perfect job she had done polishing both her fingers and toes. "Do you want to go to the all-girls school? Do you want to go live with your grandma?"

"What do I want?" she'd say, wiping her nose on her tan, bare arm, black eyeliner tears streaking down her full pretty cheeks. "I want to never have been born."

AND SO, the night came when all talk of swimming pools ended. My father came home from work, and we asked if we were going to go that night to the Anthony Pool Showroom on Ventura Boulevard, a field trip that had been greatly antici-pated for weeks, but our father shook his head and said, "We don't need a pool. We have the Houstons."

Stunned, we asked if we would ever have a swimming pool, and he shook his head again and said, "Probably not."

Then he disappeared inside his room, closed the door behind him, and changed out of his work clothes into some-thing more comfortable.

Evelyn and I were, of course, devastated. We cried. We couldn't eat. We begged our father to reconsider, but there was no penetrating the firmness of his resolve. Eventually, my mother lost all patience with us and screamed, "Just knock it off, girls! It isn't the end of the world."

And I remember my father being unusually calm that night. He seemed to savor his Schlitz in a way he rarely did. He ate with gusto. He listened to our cries of misery with a half smile on his lips and twinkle in his eyes, clearly enjoying every second of our disappointment, not so secretly pleased to have broken both of his daughters' hearts so easily.

It was a terrible night. Claiming it was my turn to control the transistor radio, I wouldn't let Evelyn listen to the Dodgers game, and to taunt her I turned up KHJ as loud as I could and sang along even louder. Clutching the radio tightly, I refused to release it even when my sister screamed right into my face with mounting desperation, "Let me have it! Let me have it! Let me have it!"

But I wouldn't. Finally she tried to grab the radio out of my hands and I kicked her away. Then she punched me and I punched her back. Then she grabbed my arm and stuck her nails so deep inside my flesh I started to bleed. I screamed and our mother came running.

The transistor radio was taken away and we were exiled to our bedroom where for the rest of the night, Evelyn and I laid on our beds on opposite sides of the room and told each other how much we hated the other and how ugly she was, and how much we hated the other and how ugly she was, until our mother finally told us once again to knock it off and just go to sleep.

WHAT MY grandfather would do when we were getting ready to leave his house after a visit was go outside and catch us some frogs. It was a simple business, almost as easy as bending down and picking up stones, there were so many of them in the grass surrounding their house. Once he trapped a few in the palm of his hand, he'd drop them into an empty Best Foods mayonnaise jar. Then, using a screwdriver, he'd punch air holes in the lid, pour in some water and a few rocks and some torn pieces of lettuce as food. The frogs were tiny, about the size of marbles, mere babies, but they moved fast inside the jar, swimming like our mother with their heads up out of the water, around and around, bumping into each other and the sides of the glass.

When we got home our mother would not let us bring the frogs inside. We had to leave them on a shelf in the garage. Then we would maybe look at the frogs the next day, but usually we forgot all about them. The little baby frogs would just never enter our minds. And we would keep forgetting for days and days and days and when we finally remembered, the frogs would, of course, be dead. There they would be, inside the mayonnaise jar, the water completely evaporated, their bodies frozen in hideous positions, legs and arms grotesquely outstretched, their tiny frog eyes open, searching to the very end for an escape that had never existed.

THREE DAYS after the killings, the police caught the nurses' murderer, and Richard Speck's ugly but somehow goofy face was everywhere. I saw his picture but could not look at it for very long. It was a murderer's face. It was what a man who killed nurses who were good, who helped you when you were sick, who knew how to give comfort and solace, looked like. But even if I never looked at Richard Speck's photo for very long, I can still picture his face perfectly, and later, after Bobbi had run away, I would think of her, somewhere on the other side of the hills that surrounded us, where in my mind, men with thin, pockmarked faces and dopey grins prowled the earth, their beady eyes ever looking for certain girls of fast cars, who laughed in the wind, their hair blowing into impossible knots behind them as they moved as far away and as fast as they could from the places they had once called home.

ENNUI

FTER THE MELANOMA WAS discovered, Harry Gifford decided he didn't want to sleep with me anymore.

"It's not personal," he explained, gripping the stick shift between us as we sat in his idling Camaro in front of my apartment building, a decaying, Spanish-style duplex on the Miracle Mile, a steady drip of cum staining my new black silk underwear, ruining them probably forever, I thought, hopelessly. "It's just that I might be, well, *dead* soon."

"Don't worry about it," I said, and tried to remember if silk was ever machine-washable as I leaned over and lightly kissed his cheek, the one with the skin cancer not on it, before getting out of his car for what I took to be the last time.

My roommate, Samantha, was exactly where I knew she would be, sitting at the kitchen table, her head turned in a funny way so she could blow smoke out the opened louvered windows behind her. I immediately noticed the half-drunk bottle of Corona but said nothing. As usual, she was wearing too much black eyeliner, so that when I walked in, she gave the false impression of being surprised.

"Gifford dumped me," I duly reported.

"Yeah?" Samantha said, and despite her wide-eyed look, the tone of her voice revealed her true lack of interest.

"Yeah. They found a deadly skin cancer on his cheek and he doesn't want to die an adulterer." I opened the refrigerator and quickly counted the remaining beers because, technically, it was *my* six-pack.

"Probably a good idea." Samantha stubbed out her cigarette and turned her attention back to the *LA Weekly* she had opened on her lap.

Using the church key we kept on a magnetic disk shaped like an old 45 of Howlin' Wolf's *Killing Floor*, I opened my beer, took a long drink, and waited to see when or if I was going to start to feel bad about being dumped.

"You want to go see the Cramps tonight?" Samantha asked, and then yawned.

"Where are they playing?"

"Starwood." Samantha finished her beer, and I hoped she wasn't going to help herself to another one, but even if she did, I knew I wouldn't say anything because, basically, I was too scared of her.

"Oh . . . I guess," I said, relieved Samantha made no move toward the refrigerator, and also I still wasn't feeling anything, but maybe a tad hungry because, if truth be told, the Harry Gifford affair was supposed to be an exercise in becoming more like Samantha, whose ennui was really the most impressive thing I had ever seen. The year was 1978. The place was Los Angeles. We weren't dumb. We knew where the key to survival lay, and it was a numbingly cold place.

HARRY GIFFORD wasn't the first teacher I ever slept with, and when he came on to me I wondered if I was getting a reputation around the Film Theory and Criticism Department, imagining the graffiti in some secret male faculty lounge that said FOR A GOOD TIME CALL SHANNON GOLD and whispered tips shared among my esteemed professors, such as "She'll give great head for a B."

"Oh, don't be silly," said my friend Curtis, a graduate student who was writing his dissertation on Dadaism in cinema (the working title being "Make Room for Dada"), when I voiced my concerns to him. "The teachers in this department can barely stand to look at one another, let alone actually speak. It's all because of Feinman. The tone is definitely set at the top."

Art Feinman, the head of the department, was a deceptively jolly-looking guy with long gray hair and a beard, who wore wrong-size pants that always seemed on the verge of falling off. I took a seminar with him once on German expressionism, and even though it was supposed to be one of those Socratic method–style deals, I don't think anyone got more than one or two words in edgewise as Feinman held forth on everything from the mise-en-scène in the opening scenes of *The Cabinet of Dr. Caligari* to the Freudian phallic symbolism of Graf Orlok's fingernails in *Nosferatu*.

"Sleep with me."

"What?" I said, looking up from the term paper Harry Gifford had just handed back during a regularly scheduled student-teacher conference at the end of the winter quarter of my junior year.

"I want you to sleep with me," he repeated, quietly but firmly, his eyes holding steady while mine shifted from picture to picture of his pretty, pale-faced wife and two small, pretty, pale-faced kids that hung on the wall behind him. My boyfriend, Tyler Fink, a guitarist with a legendary early L.A. punk band, Stunk, had just dumped me for an ex-girlfriend of one of the Rolling Stones, this amazing Teutonic beauty who was on the verge of falling over the edge into decrepitude, but who was still totally gorgeous in a scary kind of way that all rock musicians tend to find irresistible, and my already damaged self-esteem wasn't being helped by the C-minus staring up at me from the term paper I wrote on the descriptive camera angles in *Donovan's Reef*, and one thing I could say for Harry Gifford was his lectures on the non-Westerns of John Ford were never boring, which, considering the quality of the other teachers in the department, including the two I had slept with before, was actually saying a lot, and although technically he was way too preppy and normal looking to be considered my type, I did happen to think he was sexy in an older-man-of-about-thirty-eight-or-nine kind of a way, particularly his neck, which was long and nicely freckled like a small boy's, and I sort of hoped there might be some way I could improve upon my final grade, I mean, in only the most ethical way, so I took a deep breath, shrugged my shoulders, and said, "Sure."

THE TRICK was to get into clubs without paying. This was not easy because the box offices at these places were manned by chicks so hard just to look at them was like biting into a giant jawbreaker. Real teeth-splinters. I'd usually let Samantha do the talking, and just the way she was, so bored and like she didn't care one way or another if we saw the show or not, worked a lot better than my barely suppressed desperation. That's how I would get whenever I stood outside a club, desperate beyond all reason to find a way inside.

"Oh no!" I groaned when we walked around to the back of the Starwood and saw the crudely written SOLD OUT sign plastered across the window of the dark box office. My heart began to pound and my palms started to sweat.

"Jesus, Shannon. Chill," Samantha ordered, and if there was any emotion evident in her bored-to-tears voice it would've been the smallest hint of annoyance.

I looked with jealous longing at the people waiting to enter the club, most holding tickets, the magic keys that would open the doors into the only world where I could at that moment imagine wanting to be.

"Should I see if anyone has some extra tickets?" I asked, starting to talk fast as my mind shifted into panic mode. "How much money do you have? I think I left my wallet at home. But, you know, those were my beers . . ."

Samantha sighed and threw her cigarette butt onto the ground. She gave me one of her too-wide-open looks and then said exactly what I really didn't want her to say, which was "Just wait here."

I'D NEVER slept with anyone in a motel room before, I mean, a motel in my very own hometown, and it was okay except I kept thinking about an old friend of my family's who checked into a place not unlike the one Harry Gifford took me to, but instead of having a wasted afternoon of illicit sex, he just blew his brains out. If I were ever to do something like that I would check into a really nice hotel, I mean, just put it on the old credit card, right? But maybe that's the point about the final check-in, it just doesn't matter anymore, any of it.

Anyway, the motel Harry Gifford took me to was nothing to write home about, a sad little bungalow court that may have had its charm in an earlier era but now seemed to be impatiently waiting for the demolition crew to come and put it out of its misery. The first thing Harry always did upon entering the not-quite-disinfected-enough room was remove the worn bedcover, kick off his shoes, lean against the pillows, and light up one of the two or three joints he carried in his breast pocket. Since I have always hated all drugs, I never joined him and instead used the time it took Harry to get to the place he wanted, or maybe needed, to be to actually have sex with me, to review my notes from that day's classes.

Usually, we didn't talk much, which suited me just fine because I was still trying to get over Tyler Fink, who only seemed to stop talking when he was playing his guitar (not surprisingly, speed was his drug of choice), and so I found the silence to be relaxing and was not happy the day Harry Gifford broke it to ask in an oddly professorial way, given the context, "So, what exactly are your plans, Shannon?"

"Plans?" I repeated, and lowered the spiral notebook I'd filled with copious notes during my nineteenth-century Latin American history course, which was taught by a wild-haired man with Frank Zappa facial hair who always stared at my legs when I walked into class, but never met my eyes, even when he was passing back exams, on which I invariably got As.

"Yes. Plans for, shall we say, the rest of your life." Harry then smiled in that ironic way I noticed a lot of college professors smiled just to let the rest of us know that they didn't take themselves as seriously as we all knew that they actually did. Then he gasped as he struggled to keep a mouthful of marijuana smoke deep inside his lungs for a few more crucial seconds.

"Well . . . I don't know," I said, feeling the air turn strange like when you walk inside a room to take a test you have not studied for. The rest of my life was not exactly a subject I ever visited gladly.

Harry Gifford exhaled and a cloud of secondhand pot smoke caused my eyes to water momentarily, making Harry look further away than he actually was, and from this apparent distance I thought he appeared so much more attractive, like the kind of pet you would find yourself saving from the pound even if you didn't have a proper place to raise him.

"I'm only asking because I *do* care," he said with a brittle, nervous edge that brought him suddenly into sharp focus again. I was getting used to this change-of-angles thing with Harry Gifford. Ever since I'd started sleeping with him, I could not settle on a way to perceive him, which was odd. With the other teachers I had slept with, they looked to me like the same person in and out of the classroom, my feelings for them a steady hum of short-term devotion, but with Harry, he was two seemingly different people. The one going frame by frame through the opening shots of *Young Mr. Lincoln* in front of an auditorium filled with fifty note-taking students, talking with so much intimate passion about images that were not, nor ever could be, his, just would not match up with the man whose eyes never fully closed the whole time we made love.

"Well, I do, like, plan to, you know, graduate, next year," I said, the words sounding hollow even though they were totally true.

"And then?" Harry Gifford impatiently stubbed out the roach in the motel's ashtray. Like I said, this was not a particularly verbal relationship. We didn't talk, we just did, and this conversation was clearly making us both feel weird.

"Well, to tell you the truth, I don't know," I said, because, of course, that was the truth. When I thought about graduating I always had the same vision inside my head and that was of a stampede of wild horses charging through a cloud of red dust, but obviously that was not something anyone could call a plan.

"You know, Shannon, you're not dumb," he said, which really annoyed me because of course I knew that. That had never been an issue with me. It was all a matter of application, if you get what I mean. At this point, I had had enough of this conversation and so, slowly, I started to unbutton my blouse, and, as was my intention, Harry Gifford fell instantly silent and watched.

"I mean," he struggled to finish his thought, although I could tell he was no longer really thinking about my future and all the uncertainty that implied as he reached out and opened my blouse to reveal my breasts, which, I will have to tell you, were quite beautiful, perfectly rounded, and inviting to behold. Harry licked his dope-dry lips. "Perhaps you should consider going on to graduate school. A good MFA program. Maybe Madison, or even NYU. I think I could help. I mean, I would very much like to help."

"I'll consider it," I said with the firm intention of definitely not considering it, since, although a life as the ultimate voyeur (because what is Film Criticism and Theory anyway, but the science of voyeurism?) did have its allure, I also knew for a fact that that kind of permanent professional detachment tended to lead to some seriously bad behavior, the apparent universal need to compulsively fuck your own students being but one example.

Staring into what I now thought of as Harry Gifford's beautiful, stoned, black eyes, I reached out and took his warm, ever-so-slightly moist hand and placed it firmly on my left breast where, as I watched, my nipple puckered into a small insistent point, and I thought, *well, I guess this is it. He's looking for a nice way to get rid of me*, and I tried to determine how I felt about this method of sending me off to greener pastures, but Harry Gifford's finger started to oh-so-lightly tweak my nipple and I was suddenly filled with a more immediate desire.

"I really will," I lied before leaning forward to suck softly on his dry but full lower lip, the whole time listening for the sound of a single gunshot from some nearby room.

SAMANTHA WAS taking a really long time, and the more people I watched enter the Starwood the more desperate I became. It was getting close to showtime. Stray notes and high-pitched feedback began to waft out of the club and I was just about to start looking for Samantha and try to hurry this whole process along, when a car suddenly careened around a corner and up the driveway no one used because everyone knew you weren't supposed to use it and came to a screeching halt right in front of me. It was a big, fancy car, maybe a Rolls or a Bentley, one that smacked of special entitlement usually reserved for the biggest rock stars or drug dealers.

"Shannon?"

I was, of course, shocked to see Tyler Fink and his gorgeous new girlfriend emerge unsteadily from the back of the car. Tyler was very stoned. His eyes looked like they were swimming in two bloody lakes and the smile on his face was completely out of line with the rest of his features. What had I ever seen in *him*, I immediately wondered, and the only answer I could come up with was sex. But sex hadn't been bad with Harry Gifford, different, not bad, and he had just dumped me and I wasn't all distraught like I had been the day I went to Tyler's apartment and found all of my belongings sitting outside his front door in a Ralphs bag.

"Hey, like, long time no see, Shannon. Where've you been, man? Why haven't you come to any of our shows? Don't you like owe me some money?" Tyler would have gone on and on and on. Believe me, I knew him. Once he started talking he just couldn't stop, and I was about to remind him that, actually, he was the one who owed me like $300 ($300 I knew I would never see again and so hadn't really lost any sleep over), when his new girlfriend, who was staring past me at who knows what, suddenly gave him a sharp nudge in the chest.

"Who is this girl?" she demanded in a kind of way I swear I had never heard before. Yes, there was that slight German accent and the low, almost manly voice, but there was something else, something that was similar to Samantha's ennui but somehow went way beyond it.

"Oh . . . that's . . . uh . . . Shannon," Tyler said, sounding weirdly cowed—and I ask you, are guys who lead punk bands ever supposed to be cowed by anything? I mean, I thought that was the whole point, for God's sake. "You know. The girl . . . " and then he just stopped talking—him, the famous motor-mouth, rendered speechless.

"Kill her," the new girlfriend ordered in a quiet, bored, off-hand way.

"Huh?" Tyler asked, not only sounding cowed but also incredibly dumb, and I had to wonder, *how smart was he really?* I mean, his songs were all co-written by the other guys in the band, but since Tyler was the one singing I had assumed they were mostly his. I realized I should rethink that assumption.

"Kill her quickly, Tyler. She displeases me. I want her dead."

Why I continued to stand there, I cannot say. But the moment held me and I waited, breathless to see what Tyler—my boyfriend just a few short months ago, the one who always held my hand so tightly when we walked from backstage out into the night after his shows as if he were afraid he would get lost and into some serious trouble if he ever dared to let go—was going to do.

"Oh . . . gee, Eva, I don't know. I mean, shit," Tyler said, and then lazily scratched his left cheek and said nothing more, which I instantly recognized wasn't exactly a firm refusal of his girlfriend's request that he murder me.

"Oh, Jesus! You people are so—" I started, and I'm not really sure what I was going to say about them—that they were ridiculous? Stupid? Stoned? I don't know because I never got to finish, because suddenly there was a sharp pain on the side of my head as my hair was yanked so hard I screamed and lost my balance and found myself falling in this weird way to the ground.

"OW!" I hollered, too loudly, I knew, to be anyone's idea of cool, but it was as if a gallon of liquid fire had been poured straight down my right leg.

"Oh fuck," Tyler's new girlfriend said slowly, now in a dope-heavy voice that was aggravatingly foreign and familiar at the same time. She too had fallen, her sudden yank of my hair probably having caused her already questionable equilibrium to give out completely, and even though I was in excruciating pain, I was also very aware how weird it was for the two of us to be lying there, side by side on the ground outside the Starwood.

"Why the fuck did I do that?" she asked no one in particular.

"My leg," I whimpered because never in my life had I experienced what I was experiencing at that moment. "I think you broke my fucking leg."

"Did I?" The new girlfriend turned and looked at me, and we were so close, lying there really *side by side* on that hard pavement, and the look in her eyes was almost the look of a lover but without a drop of affection as she smiled a smile so dazzling that her old boyfriend in the Rolling Stones probably would've noticed it a whole sold-out stadium away.

"Cool!" she said.

"Oh God," I whined, and waited for Tyler to kneel down and surround me with comfort and concern because, well, isn't that what you're supposed to do if like someone you used to supposedly love and who had done so many sexual favors for you in some really questionable places gets hurt?

But that didn't happen, and instead he barely even looked at me as he bent down and very courteously helped his new girlfriend to her feet and, once she was standing, carefully wiped some of the gravel and dust off her ass before, without one backward glance, she strutted triumphantly away. Then, he, of course, followed.

"TYLER!" I screamed, and I guess to his credit, he did stop and turn back and look at me for I'd say a whole five seconds before he shrugged in a sheepish way and said, "Well, see ya around sometime, Shannon."

"Oh shit," I whispered, and closed my eyes and listened to someone inside the club say *test* over and over. The crowd clapped in excited anticipation and I could tell the concert was going to begin at any second. Then I heard the loose gravel crunch of approaching footsteps, and I opened my eyes to see Samantha finally returning. She stopped and looked down at me—hurt, broken, and utterly helpless—with her usual wide eyes that did not imply the slightest bit of curiosity as she reported with skull-tingling boredom, "One of the bouncers said he'll let us in if we give him and his friend blow jobs after the show. What do you say? Worth it or no?"

I FOUND out Gifford and I were on the same floor of the same hospital when I emerged from a Demerol haze to see the head of the department, Art Feinman, carrying a large bouquet of strange flowers past my door. When he glanced into my room, he stopped and stared.

"Hey," he said, and looked disconcerted and displeased at being disconcerted. "Do I know you?"

"Yeah," I said, and when he still couldn't place me, I added, "I was in your German expressionism seminar last year. You gave me a B-minus."

"A B-minus? You must've been pretty good. I don't give too many Bs, minus or otherwise. Whatcha watching?"

With a harsh tug, he attempted to lift his pants up off his hips (a hopeless gesture if I have ever seen one) and stepped inside my room, his eyes going immediately to the mounted TV on which *Double Indemnity* played.

"Great film," Feinman said, staring up at Fred MacMurray, who sat slumped in his boss's office chair, sweaty and dying, speaking into the Dictaphone, issuing his final confession, trying to make sense of his basically thrown-away life.

I stared at the flowers Art Feinman continued to hold carelessly. There was something about them that screamed *poison*. I wanted them out of my sight.

"Is he here?" I asked in a much more scared-sounding voice than I expected.

"Who?" Feinman's eyes never left the dark, dark image of the guilty man on the TV screen. But he did not have to answer. I already knew.

"Sad," I said hoarsely, with my eyes once again closed, and I felt the clouds of maybe all the horrible drugs they were giving me, but maybe it was something else, maybe it was something like despair, or perhaps not even something like despair, maybe despair was exactly what it was that consumed the entire landscape of my mind.

"Sad? This movie?" I heard Art Feinman say in his know-it-all way, but it was like I was no longer there. It was like I had already left the room. "Cynical, not sad. Big difference."

WHAT SURPRISED me was how clearly I was able to see Gifford when I hobbled over to his room a little after visiting hours officially ended. I hadn't wanted to come earlier because I was worried I might intrude on a tender little family scene. So I waited until I was fairly sure he would be alone and then stood undetected in his doorway for a while and watched him and for the first time he looked like what he probably was, a quiet, intelligent, really very decent man who had on his left cheek a discolored bandage.

"Hey. What's happening?" I finally said, claiming his attention away from *The Grapes of Wrath*, which was playing on his TV, a film we'd studied extensively in Harry's class and that I too had been watching in my hospital bed before I decided to come see him.

"Shannon?" Gifford was truly surprised to see me. But it was hard to tell if the surprise was a good or bad one.

I lifted my cast a little and said, "Guess God's punishing me for all my wicked ways."

"Yes," he said miserably, and his finger tentatively touched what looked like the damp center of his bandage. "Tell me about it."

"So, like, what's the prognosis?" I asked, I admit, nervously.

"Don't know yet. Tomorrow's the big day," he said, and then with a small backward motion of his head, beckoned me to come closer.

Awkwardly, I maneuvered with the stupid crutches into his room. On the TV, Tom Joad was telling his mother all of the places his spirit would be after he left her, and Gifford was looking at me in a way he had never done before, a way I could understand, but not quite relate to just yet. I mean, a broken leg is a broken leg. It isn't something else.

He patted his bed and moved over to make room for me, which I was actually grateful for because my leg was really beginning to hurt and what they told me to do when my leg started to hurt was to lift it. I sat down gingerly on the edge of the bed and using my hands, lifted the heavy and awkward cast up onto the mattress and then arranged myself around him. It was surprisingly easy to do, given the constraints of our situations.

"I want to kiss you," he whispered, and my eyes inadvertently fell onto the bandage on his cheek, which when seen up close did not look hopeful in the least. On the TV, in the shadowy regality of black and white, Ma Joad wept helplessly but with a kind of dignity that was only earned by a life of hardship and sorrow, and just as Harry's lips were reaching for mine, I buried my head into his once-so-alluring neck and thought about the note that our family friend left in his final moments motel room, that said '*Oh Jesus, I've had enough.*'

I reached up and gently touched the bandage on Harry Gifford's cheek and saw his lips were still waiting for mine and tried not to listen to the mournful strains of "Red River Valley" swelling on the TV's speakers, so clearly signaling the film's final frames, and said, "Please. Turn this off. I can't bear to see him go."

MATERNITY

KEVIN AND LUKE'S BABY is due any day.

"They're almost positive it's a girl," Kevin says when he calls me at work. "We're going to name her Natasha."

"Natasha's good," I say. "Then if you guys want to pretend she's a boy you can call her Nat."

"Why would we want to do that? I have no problem raising a daughter and neither does Luke," Kevin says, testily. Within about six seconds of any of our recent conversations, Kevin, one of my best and oldest friends, usually gets testy. It's because he knows I do not approve of this whole baby thing, yet he insists upon filling me in on all of the up-to-the-minute details, such as the exact shade of violet they painted the baby's room and brand and model of stroller they finally settled on after months of comparative shopping.

"Let me ask you something, Kevin," I say, and take a long sip from my Mickey Mouse mug that was given to me when I started this job at Disney eight months ago. "What if for some reason you don't like this kid? What if this baby has funny ears, or smells weird? Can you give her back?"

"To whom?" Kevin snaps.

"Her mother," I say, and bite down on my mug. Early in the day I like to hold the cup just out of sight; Mickey's open-mouthed, vaguely mocking grin tends to fill me with homicidal thoughts.

"I've told you this a million times, Lana. The baby has no mother. There is a woman, whom we do not know, who is carrying and will give birth to our child—Luke's and my child. For this service she is being paid a lot of money, and I mean a *lot*! Luke and I will be both the baby's mother and father." He pauses. "And we thought when, and if ever needed, *you* could be her female role model."

"What?" I scream, and accidentally slam my mug onto my desk. Coffee leaps over the rim and onto a pile of papers I have tried to ignore for days.

"Actually, it was Luke's idea," Kevin says. "Personally, I don't think you are the best example of womanhood."

"Thank you, Kevin." I use the edge of my sweater to mop up the spilled coffee. Even though I act fast, I can tell it's going to leave a faint stain on the thumbnail sketches for the Mickey short I have been assigned to write, "Mississippi Mickey."

"It's nothing personal, Lana. It's just the way that you are."

"And how *are* I, Kevin?"

"Oh, I don't know. I guess brittle like a Heath bar would be a good way to describe you. See, you're all crunch, Lana, and the best kind of women are more like a Mars bar. Now, even you can admit that that's true. Even you can admit that a Mars bar, you ain't."

"THE PROBLEM is you don't get Minnie," my boss, Hardy, says during the weekly staff meeting. Because other people are around he is acting tough and I think unusually cruel toward me. "You just don't get her at all."

"What don't I get?" I ask, and pick up my pen and keep it poised, really trying to be the model staff writer—ever ready and willing to learn, to improve, to please.

Quin, the animation story editor and unofficial Disneyologist, pipes in, "An excellent rule of thumb is when you write Minnie, think Carole Lombard."

Because this is said with the utmost seriousness, I keep a pensive expression on my face and jot down *Minnie = Lombard*. Then I look up and nod at Quin to let him know I got it.

Quin does nothing. He never does anything when I look at him. I think he hates me and this is why: He knows I am a poseur in their midst. Quin, who is young, straight, single, in his twenties, and almost hip—except for the Donald Duck bolo tie he wears every single day, which gives his true nerdy nature away—knows that no matter how hard I try, I will never believe in the magic of the Magic Kingdom.

"Minnie is lighter than Lombard," says Vern, an old animator who has been here so long he actually worked with Walt. "She's more, oh I don't know, *innocent*. More, more like Tweety Bird."

I solemnly nod again and cross out *Lombard* and write *Tweety*. I am starting to get that sick feeling you get when you know you've got to do something (i.e., write *Mississippi Mickey*) but also know, just know, you're going to fail even before you do it.

My boss, actually the head of the animation department, so he's everybody in the room's boss, Hardy, impatiently begins to tap his pen on the table. He looks at his watch and says, "All right . . ."

That is his signal for the meeting to end. Hardy is not good at disguising his boredom, and he gets bored easily.

"But if Minnie's Tweety Bird," Jody, another staff writer, asks earnestly, clearly missing Hardy's cue, "then who exactly is Mickey?"

"Oh Jesus," Hardy moans, and throws his pen into the air and it appears to land accidentally in my lap. It is one of those novelty pens, the type that if you tilt it the right way the top part of a bosomy woman's bathing suit falls down to reveal a pair of very impressive tits. Without saying anything, Hardy has just informed me that our "lunch" date is still on.

"Mickey is nothing but a sexless little shit," Hardy says, and the room goes silent. No one, and I mean no one, laughs.

"I'm joking, of course," Hardy says quickly and a little bit too loudly as his eyes move guiltily around the room, making contact with everyone's but mine.

FROM THE window of the bedroom of Hardy's temp housing apartment conveniently located a few blocks from the studio, I look down at the swimming pool. Because it is overcast and the middle of the week, there is only one person down there: a very pregnant woman who is dressed in shorts and a large sweatshirt. She dangles her feet in the water and reads a magazine.

I wonder if she is the woman carrying Kevin's and Luke's baby. I wonder that every time I see a pregnant woman these days.

Hardy moved to L.A. eleven months ago when he took the job at Disney, but he left his wife and kids in New Jersey. It is not clear when or if his family will join him out here. When I ask about this, he gives me vague and conflicting answers. Even though I can accurately be called many unflattering things, a home-breaker is not one of them. I actually hope Hardy's marriage can survive this separation. Like my job at Disney, I know that this relationship is only temporary. Although Hardy and I are roughly the same age, we seem to come from different generations, and the gap between us is substantial. An example of our differences is the fact he can stand to live in a place like this. Technically, it is a nice apartment, I guess, but there is something awful about it; it's bland but somehow taunting. I truly hope Hardy will return to his wife soon, if only to pry him out of this dreadful place.

I hear the front door open and look up to see Hardy rush into the bedroom as if he is afraid someone is following him. He makes no acknowledgment of my presence as he throws his keys and wallet onto the bedside table and then collapses on the bed, dramatically throwing an arm over his face.

"I'm fucked," he groans. "I am really fucked!"

"Gee, it's great to see you too, loverboy," I say, and squeeze the toe of his expensive Italian loafer that he has not bothered to remove. Then I start to close the curtains.

"They hate Miss Bianca," Hardy says from under his arm. "They hate Bernard. They want more emotion in the film!"

The film in question is the latest *Rescuers* movie. Miss Bianca and Bernard are a couple of mice, but they're nothing like Mickey and Minnie. They don't even appear to come from the same species. That's okay in animation; you can have species within species.

I look out the window once more. The pregnant woman has cast aside the magazine and is inching her way into the water. Slowly, I close the curtain and notice that Hardy's wallet lies open on the table beside me, and I can see the pictures he still carries with him—the ones of his wife and children. Obviously, I have never met Connie or the kids. The photos in the wallet are small and subdued; his daughter, Gretchen, looks like she has been crying, and his son, Chris, has an angry glint in his eyes as if he's ready to belt somebody. Connie is pretty and blond and seems to be looking pointedly away from her unhappy children.

"This is it," Hardy whines from the bed. "My days are numbered now."

Before my job at Disney the only scripts I had ever written were the ones for the kind of experimental/autobiographical video pieces that I wrote, directed, starred in, and produced using money I had begged and borrowed from everybody and anybody. One of the videos (the least successful of the six) was about my relationship with my fucked-up grandparents, but the other five were all about my relationships with my fucked-up boyfriends. They were, shall we say, kind of sexually explicit, and I think it was because of all of the explicit sex that they attained a cult following and were routinely shown in midnight screenings at arty coffeehouses, university experimental cinema classes, and quite a few fraternity house rumpus rooms.

Besides attracting a lot of very weird and sick fan mail, eventually my videos attracted the attention of a pretty big Hollywood agent.

"I love you," she gushed in an embarrassing way. "Everybody at this agency loves you. Your wish is our command."

"I need money," I said.

"You need a job, huh?"

"No," I corrected. "I have a job. I make my films. I just need money to make them."

"Got it," she said, and then I didn't hear from her for weeks.

"They love you at Disney," she said when she finally did call.

"They do?" I could not hide my skepticism. "*Disney* wants to pay for my films?"

"No, silly," she laughed. "They want you to write for their animation department."

"Excuse me?"

"Cartoons. Daffy Duck. It's a cinch."

"But why would they want *me* to do *that*?"

"They don't. Hardy does. And he is all that matters."

"But I don't want to write cartoons."

"Just meet Hardy," she persevered. "He saw the videos and he loves you."

"But why would some guy who works in animation love *me*?"

"Guess," the big Hollywood agent said.

"Hardy, honey," I say, and sit back down beside him on the bed.

He has not moved at all. His arm still covers his face. The soft brown leather shoes still cover his feet. An air of gloom hangs over both of us. "You want to forget this today? I mean, it's okay with me. I'm actually feeling a little hungry anyway . . ."

"What?" Hardy says in a totally distracted way.

Like a prince in the animated films, Hardy is very handsome and has a really great jaw. It is kind of large and well shaped and always perfectly smooth. There is never any stubble. But his neat looks are deceptive. I have discovered to my delight, sexually speaking, there is nothing well pressed about him.

I lean back on the pillow beside him but do not touch. One of the bad things that happens after you've watched yourself making love on film is that you become very self-conscious about your lovemaking. I mean, I often wonder if I am touching a person the way that I am touching him because it is what I want to do, or if I'm doing it because I know how good it looked when I touched somebody like that on film. I have to get totally swept away with true passion before I can close that inner eye, the filmmaker's eye, the one that, even though I haven't made a movie in over a year, still seems always to be watching.

"Let me ask you a question, Hardy," I say. "Do you think two homosexual men can really be good parents to a little girl?"

"Oh, I don't know!" Hardy says from under his arm. "Lana, my job is on the line. I am probably lying on my deathbed, so to speak, and may I point out that if I go, you're definitely out of there, too."

"I don't care," I say, and against my will, one of my hands reaches over and lightly begins to trace the outline of that perfect jaw.

"You should care," Hardy says, and the tips of my fingers travel over one of his cheeks to feel the warmth of his lips, the wetness of his mouth. Gently, they press themselves inside, and his lips close around them. He begins to suck softly.

"You're right, Hardy. I should care, but that's why you hired me, isn't it?" I say, and press my body against his. I can feel my breath collecting inside my chest; it feels almost like loneliness but it's not.

"You hired me because . . ." I whisper into his ear, "you saw the things I could do. You saw who I really am . . ."

Finally, his arm lifts and wraps itself around my neck and pulls me closer than I already am. His mouth opens slightly and my fingers slip out and slide down his neck, over his torso, reaching.

"Who are you, really?" he asks, his dark eyes looking into my dark eyes.

"I am," I whisper, feeling him quickly grow under my stroking hand. "Cinderella's lost glass slipper . . . You saw me waiting . . . to be filled."

I RUN into Luke and Kevin at the dog park. It is twilight, the park's busiest time, and there are dogs and owners everywhere. Kevin and Luke have brought Murray and Mitzu, their Pomeranians, to frolic, but only under their watchful eyes. A few months ago a Great Dane killed a miniature poodle, just picked it up and shook until the poodle's neck snapped.

"She's in labor," Kevin tells me, his eyes blazing with uncontained excitement. "The baby's coming!"

"Cool," I say, halfheartedly, and Kevin shoots me an annoyed look that I ignore.

"God, I just hate coming here," Luke complains, and checks the bottom of both of his shoes, seemingly unfazed by his pending parenthood. "But if we keep the dogs cooped up all day, they drive us nuts at night."

"They drive *you* nuts, darling," Kevin corrects. "They never bother me. I could sleep though a blitzkrieg."

"Try a screaming infant," I say, pointedly. My dog, Ferus, is making a fool of himself, running around like a maniac, barking and intimidating the shyer dogs. I pretend I do not know him.

"Don't worry, Lana. I'll make sure Kevin does not miss a moment of that fun," Luke says. He is probably ten years younger than Kevin and me, in his midtwenties and quite a doll, your perfect California dream boy. If he were straight, I would devour him in an instant. Kevin knows he really lucked out when he landed Luke and can barely keep from gloating.

Kevin releases Murray and Mitzu and they immediately start to scamper down the hill and out of our sight. Luke runs off after them, and Kevin gives me an appraising look.

"Well, you certainly appear . . . refreshed, Lana. I bet you had a very nourishing 'lunch' today."

"Oh, leave me alone, Kevin," I warn. "For all intents and purposes, I am currently standing on the edge of certain self-destruction."

Kevin smiles appreciatively like I knew he would. He isn't a particularly good-looking guy. He has a pug nose and beneath his neatly trimmed mustache is a scar from an operation that corrected a harelip, but as always he is beautifully dressed, today all in immaculate tennis whites, although I know for a fact he does not play. What he does is direct commercials and very big-budget commercials at that. For this he gets paid a buttload of money but is always complaining about his unfulfilled artistic dreams. I think that is why he sought out my friendship. He would like to make the small, personal, noncommercial films that I used to make but can't anymore because I don't have the money he does to make them.

"How does one not feel like a prostitute?" I ask, and notice both of my shoelaces have somehow come untied.

"Maybe by not sleeping with your boss for starters," Kevin says. "But to tell you the truth, Lana, it's a little hard for me to concentrate on this little problem of yours because I am having a baby this very second."

"Look, Kevin, lend me a little money. Not much. Just a little, so I can quit my job and start another film. I'll pay you back when . . ."

"Sorry, Lana," Kevin looks around, and his gaze settles instinctively upon Luke, who is carrying the dogs back up the hill. "I'd like to, but I've got a family to consider now, and your shoes are untied."

"Here," Luke forcefully places both dogs into Kevin's arms. "Your turn."

Even though Kevin tells the dogs repeatedly to stay near, the second he puts them back onto the ground, they once again start to scamper down the hill. This time, Kevin gives chase, and I can't help but notice that his gait is nowhere near as graceful as Luke's.

"I wish we never started this whole thing," Luke says as soon as we are alone.

"Bringing the dogs to the park?" I ask, and spot Ferus raising his leg and peeing on an unattended picnic basket. I look away.

"No. The baby," Luke continues to speak quietly. "Lana, look at our dogs, for God's sake. Have you had a good look at them lately? They're neurotically eating themselves alive. What is going to happen to our poor child?"

"What does Kevin say?" I ask, and watch Kevin at the bottom of the hill, hovering close to the two dogs, standing protectively near.

"He says children are different and everything is going to be fine. But I don't believe him. I don't think things are going to be fine ever again."

I glance over at Luke's cool, perfect beauty. Both Kevin and Luke gave sperm samples so they would not know whose child it really was. Considering the incalculable value of beauty in our society, I hope for the baby's sake that it was one of Luke's sperm cells that hit the bull's-eye.

"You'll help us, won't you, Lana?"

"Help how?"

"With the baby."

"I know nothing about caring for babies."

"I'm not talking about knowledge. I'm talking about instincts," Luke says, and bends down and begins carefully to tie both of my shoes.

"Luke, you know what my instincts tell me to do when I see a baby? Run!"

"God, I know," Luke says, and sighs. "So do mine."

THE TEAHOUSE rocks in the Santa Ana wind and I think about the old Disney cartoon of the three little pigs. I can't tell you for sure which piggy built this house, but something tells me it wasn't the patient, industrious one.

I live in an authentic Japanese teahouse with movable rice paper walls and my own bamboo garden—one of six such teahouses situated on a rustic hillside in Echo Park. It is very quiet and eerily beautiful here, but to get to the houses, you must take a long, unlit dirt footpath, and at night—particularly when it's windy—it can be kind of spooky.

For my entire adult life I have lived alone (I don't consider Ferus to be much of a roommate; our arrangement is more like that of co-habitants, except I am the co-habitant who provides the food, water, medical care, and anything else the dog might need). One of my videos started with an ex-boyfriend, the famous stunt pilot Cooper Epstein, asking me to move into his condo in Santa Monica with him. Then other things happen, like a local punk band hiring me to direct a music video but only after I promise to give the lead singer head. In the next part of the film, I bore all of my friends by endlessly going over the pros and cons of moving in with Cooper, who, at the end of the piece, finds out about the singer and tells me that not only does he not want to live with me, but also that he might strangle me if he ever lays eyes on me again.

I lie on my futon and close my eyes and feel my house quake with each new gust of wind. I have to turn in my script for *Mississippi Mickey* at the end of the day tomorrow. It is going to be on everyone's weekend read. I haven't even started it yet. To get myself in the mood I've read and reread both *Huck Finn* and *Tom Sawyer*, but every time I sit down to write, my mind wanders and I find myself fantasizing about something or other. Okay, I'll admit it, about sex.

"What is sex like with a long-term monogamous partner?" I asked Kevin once.

"Safe," he had said.

I am not happy with my failure to make this job, my first and only real one, work. I tried. Or, at least, I think I tried, but it was like I was coated in Crisco. I just couldn't make myself stick in the normal workaday world. I have a hard time with that in general. I'm always slipping out of situations. I'm always sliding away.

Hardy knows I tried, that I really, really tried, and I think he is genuinely sorry the job hasn't worked out for me.

"You have talent, Lana," he told me one day over a real lunch at the Disney commissary. "But you're just too fucking self-involved to use it in any marketable way."

The phone rings and, since it is late, I am sure it is Hardy.

"I'm yours," I whisper because I know that is what he wants to hear and also because it is the truth, for at least that moment.

"No, you most certainly are not. Thank God." It takes me a moment to recognize who is speaking.

"Luke," I say. "What's up?"

"She's here," Luke says. "Natasha's here."

"The baby?"

"Oh, Lana," Luke says, and then quietly starts to cry.

"What's wrong?" I ask, feeling nervous.

"Kevin went to the hospital. There's been some kind of problem . . ."

"What kind of problem?" I ask, even more scared.

"The birth mother disappeared."

"Disappeared? With the baby?"

"No. No. She left the baby, but she just disappeared right after the delivery and now no one knows what to do," Luke says, still sniffling. "Kevin wanted me to come with him to help straighten this whole mess out, but I told him I was catching a cold and shouldn't be spreading germs around a maternity ward, which was a complete lie. So, Lana, you have to go there."

"What?" I say, shocked.

"Kevin needs support. He shouldn't be dealing with this all by himself."

"But, Luke, you're his partner," I say, and rub my eyes. My head has started to throb. A gust of wind whips up, and I hear a few stalks of bamboo in my garden snap. I think of an opening image for *Mississippi Mickey* a riverboat caught in a tumultuous storm.

"Lana, listen to me," Luke starts softly, but his voice grows stronger. "I . . . I haven't even seen this goddamn baby and I already hate her guts."

"Oh, Luke, don't say that."

"It's just . . ." I can tell Luke has started to cry again. "I'm just so afraid she's going to take Kevin away from me."

"That's normal. Those kinds of fears. That's what new parents go through all the time. It's normal, Luke."

"Lana," Luke says wearily. "You know and I know there is nothing normal about this situation at all."

It is after three in the morning when I get to the hospital, and as soon as the elevator doors open I see Kevin, for once not beautifully dressed, in an ill-fitting sweat shirt and badly wrinkled shorts, standing alone in one of the delivery rooms. In his arms he holds a small, quiet bundle.

"What are you doing here?" he says when he sees me.

67

"I've come to deliver a baby. Didn't I tell you I was pregnant?" I say, and for a second, because he is so confused and agitated, it looks like he believes me.

"I'm kidding, Kevin. Let me see her."

"Who?" he asks, utterly at a loss.

"Your daughter," I say, and for the first time he smiles and oh, what a smile; it is one that covers a thousand miles in a millisecond.

Gently, he leans down and presents her to me. She's all bundled up in a soft yellow blanket and I can only see her face. It is very pink and round. Her lips are just a bit darker than the rest of her skin and her eyebrows and lashes are so fair they are invisible. I think she has Kevin's pug nose but remember that all babies have squashed noses and there's still hope hers will change.

"She's really something," is all I can think to say.

"Isn't she?" Kevin whispers almost like a lover into my ear.

Silently, we gaze at her. She does almost nothing, but still, every twitch is amazing. Her forehead wrinkles, lips purse, eyes roll around.

"Mr. Canton," a woman says in a high, sweet voice, and Kevin wrenches his gaze away from his daughter and looks at the small Filipino nurse who has just entered the room. "The resident can see you now."

"Oh, thank God, finally," Kevin grumbles, and without warning, puts the baby into my arms. "Everything is so fucked up, Lana. I have to sign like a billion forms before they can give this poor child her first bottle. Can you believe a woman would just disappear after delivering her child?"

"It's not *her* child, remember?" I say, and try to adjust my arm so that the baby is comfortable and start to pray that she doesn't begin to do something, like cry.

"Cradle her head and don't let her slip out of your arms, Lana," Kevin instructs before he leaves me all alone with the kid.

Obediently, I hold the baby a little tighter. She is warm and perfectly quiet. I have never held a newborn before, and I don't know what I'm supposed to do but just hope that whatever it is I am doing isn't too horribly wrong.

For the first time I get a look at my surroundings. The maternity ward has been decorated with painted images of Disney characters. They're all here, Mickey, Minnie, Donald, Goofy, even Tinker Bell. Personally, these are not the images I would choose to welcome a child into the world, and even though I know they say newborns can't see, I hold Natasha closer.

Kevin once pointed out that all of my films ended with a similar shot, one of me standing alone—inside an abandoned train station, outside a blazing Mexican dance hall, next to a dried-up creek bed, somewhere.

"Lonely are the ones who do not know how to love," he said to me, I thought, kiddingly.

A handsome young man dressed all in hospital greens walks hurriedly down the hallway. When he passes, he looks into the room and smiles at me and I wonder if he thinks I'm the child's mother. The child's poor mother. Where could she have gone? She, who is also like Cinderella's glass slipper, but the other one, the one the Prince did not find. The one that just disappeared when the carriage became a pumpkin and the white horses plain field mice.

"Beware the stroke of midnight," I whisper conspiratorially to Natasha, and even though I know she cannot comprehend the words I have just spoken, her sightless eyes focus on my face and lock in what I imagine to be a rare second of complete, if unspoken, understanding.

TIGER BEAT

GOT PAID FOR it once. Not officially. He called it cab fare. Sure, $200 cab fare. Some ride. The four $50 bills floated loosely around my purse for days like playful devils popping up unexpectedly when I groped for my keys, lip gloss, chewing gum—only a whisper, *boo*, but still loud enough to scare the living daylights out of me. Just thinking about that night with that man made me feel lightning-struck—unscathed on the outside but fried to a burnt bacon crisp within. I spent the money on new tires, four of them: Firestones that hummed on the road, a high-pitched wail that I thought would go away after they lost their newness, and they did get quieter, but I still heard it, an exhaustless sigh like the sounds we make when our minds inadvertently drift to scenes of natural disaster, displays of total devastation.

HARPER SAW the gray hair first and pulled it out without asking, a tiny white ping on the top of my head. He held it in front of my face, between my eyes so I had to cross them slightly, and I still couldn't really see it.

"Look, Lita. You've started to fade," Harper teased.

"Let me see," I said, and reached for the hair, but Harper let it go and together we watched it float dreamily down toward the trailer's floor, suspended for a few seconds in a slanting ray of bright morning light.

"You know, I'm not afraid of growing old," I told Harper for the forty-millionth time, and for the forty-million-and-first time, he smiled and said, "But honey, you really should be."

THEY WERE much older—ten, twelve, fourteen years my senior—always an even number for some reason. Men in their early, middle, and late thirties, most single, the skin on their backs just begining to loosen. They would pick me up hitchhiking and were anxious to tell me about their pasts, glass bowls filled with spent candy wrappers carelessly wadded up. Some sported mustaches and smoked cigarettes. Others wore pants too low on their expanding hips. The absolute worst reeked of expensive cologne. They bought me ice cream cones, jamocha almond fudge, mint chip, pralines and cream. I never shared, not even a lick. The best part was getting into their cars for the first time, feeling the air thicken with possibility as I stared straight ahead out the windshield, ready, expecting, hoping to be shattered by the smallest touch, not knowing what the engine was going to sound like, or how this one would take hold of the wheel.

I MET Harper much later, long after that stage in my life when, as my mother likes to say, I was a different person. Ironically, Harper picked me up the same way as the others, but his car was not like theirs. It wasn't even a car; it was an old truck, mud splattered, with questionable shock absorbers. In the past, my destination had never been important. It was the rides that mattered and the opportunities they afforded. But the day Harper picked me up, I was definitely going somewhere.

"Reseda. To my mother's house. She's having a bad reaction to some new thyroid medicine and can't get out of bed. I'm worried and my car is in the shop, so . . ." I was shocked to hear these words come out of my mouth because they were true. In the past I revealed as little about myself as possible and the things I did tell those older men were usually lies.

"I'll take you there," Harper said without hesitation.

"Really?" I looked at him carefully for the first time. Harper was about my age (thirty) and beautiful. His long blond hair blew off of his face, exposing a net of fine lines around his eyes that made him look both ironic and wise. His offer surprised me. The goal of all those other men had always been just to get me into their cars. The point was to watch me close the door.

"Really." Harper smiled, and his teeth were straight and white, and the pale blue fabric of his well-washed T-shirt looked as if it would feel velvety against my hand. Coming through the truck's radio was the Beach Boys song "Wouldn't It Be Nice."

Like a fool—because what are we, when we find ourselves falling instantly in love with a complete stranger, but utterly helpless fools?—I smiled back at Harper and asked, "Are you really, *really* sure?"

Harper didn't answer. He didn't need to. I was to learn that his certainty in all things has never needed reaffirmation.

THERE WAS the one who dripped hot sealing wax on my belly. Always in artistic patterns, vivid colors, imperial blue, pine green, magenta. He whispered to me. Said things that made me not dare look at him, things that might have made me smirk if I didn't want so much to believe. The pain was nothing really. It happened and then it was over, like felt-covered mallets hitting metal chimes. I wanted more. "Hush," he ordered before placing bone-dry kisses beside the drops of hardening wax.

ON THAT first ride to my mother's house, I learned that Harper was a farmer who grew organic bananas on a small plot of land just south of Ventura.

"I didn't know bananas could grow in Southern California," I shouted, because Harper's truck had no air conditioning and once we had descended into the hot, smoggy valley, we had to keep our windows rolled all the way down.

"Technically, they can't," he shouted back, and then nodded proudly to himself. "But I'm doing it."

"You're magic," I yelled, completely awed.

"No," he yelled, and shook his head. "Just stubborn."

MY MOTHER knew about the older men and she was worried. Once she told me I was not made of Teflon, that everything I did was going to stick. I laughed.

"This is because of your father, isn't it?" my mother had then asked, guiltily.

"Without question," I said, and laughed again.

HARPER AND I went on dates, actual dates: to the movies, to hear music, to dance, to the beach in winter where we lay on the cold sand and talked for hours. Then, finally, one night in the thatched hut he constructed by hand in the far corner of the banana field (that's right, *a thatched hut*), lit only by the cold white light of a Coleman lantern, he ran his fingers for the first time over my body, as if searching for bruises, black spots just beneath the skin. I stared up into his blue eyes and said, "I won't lie to you."

"Please," he said. "Please do."

MY FEET were not quite touching the ground. I was traveling on a different plane than most. Sometimes I wondered how exactly I had arrived there and was superstitious about crashing. I avoided mirrors; all reflective surfaces made me look away. I tried wearing only shoes with soft soles and never slept with any of the older men more than four times. You could depend upon the first three to be different, somehow off-balance, but usually the fourth marked the beginning of a routine, the pulling out of landing gear, tires hitting the ground at impossible speeds, but then, of course, always screeching to an inevitable stop.

WITHIN A year of our meeting, I moved in with Harper on the banana farm. The hut was too small for the two of us and so we bought a used Airstream trailer from a retired naval officer in Point Mugu. I brought my Cuisinart with me along with a cold, calculating head for business. Harper planted more trees, filling the entire ten acres with different varieties of bananas. Together we slowly made the business a success.

"Bet never in your wildest dreams did you ever see yourself ending up a farmer's wife, Lita," Harper once said happily, proudly, as if he had personally pulled off a sneaky trick on fate.

I squeezed his hand a little tighter. We were walking beneath the trees in the cooling breeze of a warm September night and I was holding a flashlight that only illuminated a small circle of dirt path ahead of us. It was true that like the banana trees, I was somehow thriving in this hitherto unimaginable place, but the fact that I could not have imagined it did not surprise me. I have never been able to see very far into the future. I have only been able to see what is right before me. And, of course, what is behind.

THERE WERE dry spells, times I considered lowering my standards only to realize I had none. I took long baths and fantasized about dead movie stars, not the obvious tragically doomed ones like James Dean, but rather the guys who simply grew old and died: Spencer Tracy, Edward G. Robinson, Hank Fonda. I even became slightly fixated upon Joseph Cotten for a short while before I learned that he was still alive and that, of course, ruined him for me completely.

LATELY I find myself thinking a lot about the animals that mate for life, the species we speak of with such reverence.

"I wonder," I asked Harper one night, "if geese ever have regrets."

"Animals don't think that way." Harper's voice rose confidently out of the darkness. He was lying close, but we were not touching. Outside the trailer the night was quiet; fog moved in uncharted currents. I turned on my side and looked at him and thought as I had countless times before how handsome he was, really, like a statue, solid and well chiseled. He, too, lay on his side, eyes wide open, watching me. I wanted to kiss him but didn't, realizing that what I really wanted was for him to kiss me.

"But what if they have all kinds of thoughts that we can't tell because we only see their behavior?" I asked, and reached out and felt the wall behind the bed, the one that seemed to be closing in on us, making the already-tight space feel even tighter. "And behavior can be very misleading, can't it?" I asked.

"Sometimes, yes," he said, and suddenly grabbed my hand, stopping it from its determined but impossible task of pushing the wall out to give us more room to breathe. "Sometimes, no."

I BROKE the four-time rule for the one who made love to me in his sleep. I woke up in the middle of the night to find him shifting my legs, but with his eyes firmly closed. He did it differently than before, his movements ghostlike and probing. I was fascinated. The next morning he had no recollection of what we had done, but he didn't seem surprised, either. I slept with him three more times, six in all, but much to my disappointment, he never stirred in his sleep again.

HARPER KEEPS charts. He maps out the projective fruit-bearing cycles of his trees. He watches the sun and experiments with different kinds of fertilizer, varied amounts of water, always trying to find natural ways to produce more and better product.

I do our books, and also those of the organic orange growers in Ojai and the lovely Japanese American farmer who grows edible flowers in a giant hothouse a little bit south of here in Oxnard. I find that I like working with figures because you can count on every equation having an end.

Sometimes, I watch Harper draw his neat arrows, always pointing back and around with no end in sight. He keeps his blond hair pulled back into a loose ponytail and a serious expression on his face.

"You are a good man to be with," I tell him, and kiss the top of his head.

"Why?" he asks without looking up from his work.

"Because you are a man with faith," I say, and then stand there with both hands on his shoulders, waiting for some reassurance that Harper's improbable faith in *me* remains intact. But he says nothing and I watch as he draws another arrow, this one pointing once again back to the beginning of the chart.

THEN THERE was the teen idol, the pinup guy in those magazines, *16*, *Fave*, *Tiger Beat*. I didn't meet him hitchhiking. I met him in a club. He was short enough to stand under a low shelf without crouching. I didn't recognize him, but back at his hotel the coffee table was covered with fan mail.

"How old are you?" I asked.

"Too old to be who I am."

Later, I got out of bed and read some of the letters. Big mistake. They were from young girls, ten, twelve, fourteen years old. Some sent pictures, school headshots, overlit, posed in front of phony backdrops. The girls were not pretty. Their bangs were cut too short, their chins were too small, their glasses unbecoming. These were not letters from the popular girls, but messages from the outside. Most of the notes were short and cheerful enough, telling about their pets and invitations to birthday parties and the grades on their report cards, but one was unusually long and written on a plain piece of soft white paper. The accompanying picture was of a middle-aged man with protruding front teeth and round rosy cheeks, the chipmunk face of the girl's father who, she said, had died recently in a car crash. "My father's death has made my heart ache," the girl wrote. "It has become increasingly difficult for me to feel the same way for you as I did before. I am sorry. I hope you can forgive me." The girl had drawn a string of crudely shaped hearts connected with what looked like a barbed wire vine along the bottom of the page.

I stared at the photo of the girl's father and thought about my own. If my father had died in a car crash when I was younger, I was certain my heart would not have retreated to an untouchable spot behind a barbed wire fence. My heart would have broken loose, soared, finally free. I thought of how different my life could have been, the choices I would certainly not have made. When the teen idol called for me to come back to bed, I was startled and the photo of the girl's father fell out of my hand. He called for me again, but it was too late. I was already hurrying out the door.

SOME AFTERNOONS, I take a break from bookkeeping and carry my tea out to the steps of the trailer where I sit and look out at the neat rows of banana trees heavily laden with green unripe fruit. The workers Harper hires are mostly young Latinos who in the heat of the day strip off their shirts and tie them, turban-style, around their heads. The skin on their backs is taut and a deep roasted color. I watch them among the straight trees with interest. At thirty-four, I think I can start to understand what I looked like to those older men of my past, how the view changes with time, becoming somehow more focused and inevitably predatory.

THERE WERE things I never did, corny stuff like sex in hot tubs, oral in cars. And I never got paid for it except for that one time, but that was near the end, very soon after the night with the teen idol.

For me, settling down with Harper was like finally returning home.

When I told Harper this, I felt compelled to add, "But then, you have to ask yourself, why did Odysseus leave in the first place if all he ever wanted to do was come back?"

Harper took a sip of the beer we were sharing and thought about this a second before he said, "I guess he had to."

"But, Harper," I, for some reason, persisted. "If life is really cyclical, does that mean we have to leave again and again?"

Harper didn't say anything. He handed me the beer but I didn't drink. Of course, I knew the answer to my question was yes. We do have to leave again and again, even if we don't want to, even if all we want is to stay where we are and find a way to make our lives work. I knew the answer, but wanted, perhaps needed, to hear Harper say it. But he just reached over and took the beer back from me and said, "I don't know, Lita. I never got to the end of that book."

MY MOTHER once asked me if I ever missed any of them.

"Miss any of who?" I said.

LATE AT night, Harper has started to talk to me about farming, I think to encourage fertile thoughts. He believes that having kids is the obvious next phase of our lives, the logical summation of our equation. But we have been trying to conceive for two years now with no success. Whenever I'm ready to admit defeat, Harper reminds me of all of the times he was told bananas would never grow in Southern California. Still, it is hard for him to contain his disappointment. And I am loath to keep disappointing him. The question that haunts me is, *How much faith can anyone have in another person, really?*

What I've found is it is hard for me to think about sex in a life-producing way—mainly, I think, because for all those years it was something else, almost the opposite. What I was trying to do was lessen my load, make my body melt into puddles of sweat, give something up with each orgasm, not much, perhaps just another unsettled wisp from my young and restless and never-to-be-satisfied soul.

I look at my belly, no longer flat, now a slightly loosened sail, and think of the elements, earth, sun, and water, and try to figure out how to change my behavior again, how I could learn to move, no longer like the shifting sands of some barren oasis, but maybe slither like thick gooey mud, undulate like a primeval stew.

IN ITS PLACE

THIS IS HOW IT started:

I was walking the dog along a path near my house when I slipped on a patch of black ice. It wasn't a bad fall, but the pain was sharp, and when I looked down I saw my jeans had ripped and a nasty-looking, barklike scrape across my knee was beginning to exude tiny droplets of blood. My fiercely beating heart beat harder. Just that morning I had read an article in the *Times* about these new antibiotic-resistant bacteria and now I, either through sheer carelessness or bad luck, had managed to provide a perfect opening for those potentially deadly germs.

I got to my feet, called the dog, and started back, anxious to get home as quickly as possible and put some disinfectant on my wound, but as fast as I walked it did not seem fast enough. It would probably take about fifteen minutes and during those fifteen minutes there would be no line of defense between me and the potentially deadly bacteria. Fifteen minutes was actually a long time. Bacteria move very quickly (this I did not actually know—I was just guessing) and the seeds of my demise could already be firmly in place before I even reached my front door. Then I noticed my knee ached with each step and I was walking slower than usual. It was going to take longer than fifteen minutes. Maybe as long as twenty or twenty-five, which was, of course, almost half an hour. One half of an hour and there are only twenty-four hours in a day and three hundred and sixty-five days in a year and I had just celebrated my forty-seventh birthday and forty-seven seemed like kind of a paltry number when you considered it a whole life.

The risk I was taking with each additional second I knew to be unacceptable. Unacceptable! But what could I do? I wasn't going to get home any faster. Desperately, I began to gaze at the windows of the houses that lined the path, searching for any signs of life, deciding that when I spotted an occupied house I would rush around to the front door, ring the bell, and ask those occupants, those, well, *strangers* for help. But the windows were all dark. No one appeared to be home. *Where could everybody be?* I wondered in frustration. Someone had to be home in this neighborhood—a bored parent playing a repetitive game with a small child, a nice, retired couple silently reading the morning paper together at the kitchen table, or maybe some self-employed person such as myself (I was a freelance cookbook editor who worked—when I had work, which I hadn't for a while—out of a home office). *Someone.* But every house I passed appeared cloaked in the same shadowy vacancy.

Then I saw it, my eleven-year-old son's best friend Lyle's house. I knew his house would most likely be empty too. His parents were both architects and worked long days in D.C. firms, and Lyle was, of course, in school with my son, Max, but Max had once told me that Lyle's family kept a spare house key under the mat inside the unlocked screen porch and whenever I passed their house I always thought about that key. It, for some reason, lurked stubbornly in the back of my mind.

For courtesy's sake, I did knock on Lyle's back door. An obviously wasted gesture that to my consternation ate up quite a few precious seconds. I could tell no one was home. There was just this deep, silent heaviness that indicated a definite absence of life. So, with fingers slightly shaking with mounting impatience, I lifted the mat, and spotted the key exactly as I had always imagined it, sitting there, waiting almost expectantly to be taken into my hand.

It was not the first time I had ever been inside Lyle's house. I had come a few times to pick up Max, but never stayed long. We were still pretty new to the area and did not know many people, but I liked Lyle's parents, the architects. The mother, who was Chinese, was very nice and welcoming to my son, and the father, a Caucasian, was always friendly in a low-key but seemingly open-to-anything kind of a way. I had been meaning to invite them to dinner but hadn't yet.

The house was one of the standard models of our subdivision—a colonial—but unlike other colonials that I noticed tended to have small rooms crammed with too much furniture, Lyle's parents had knocked down walls and made the downstairs a more "open" floor plan, and the furnishings were spare. There was a nice, as they say, "flow" to the house, and almost as if swept along by an invisible current, I found myself racing through the den, into the entrance hall, and up the stairs to Lyle's bathroom, where I swung open the medicine cabinet and grabbed a tube of Neosporin, a bottle of hydrogen peroxide, a spray can of Bactine, and a box of Band-Aids.

First, I poured some hydrogen peroxide on my wound, then spread a fairly thick frosting of Neosporin over it, and finally sprayed the whole area with a cool mist of Bactine before carefully placing a large (but better too big than too small, I figured) Band-Aid (this one festooned with characters from *The Simpsons*) over my knee. Staring down at a gaping Homer, I felt the ribs around my chest begin to relax and my breath come easier. It was too soon to know, of course. I would definitely have to keep a close eye on that knee in the days to come, but I was pretty confident I had prevented anything too awful from creeping inside me. I was *pretty* confident about that.

I got up from the toilet where I had sat (in my impatience, without even closing the seat!) and was just about to put everything away when, for the first time, no longer in a paranoid, hyperventilating panic, I was able to take notice of *the supreme orderliness of the medicine cabinet*. It was absolutely amazing. On the top shelf were only bottles, all nearly the same size and placed at a slight angle, like dancers in a chorus line just before they executed a dramatic, synchronized about-face. Their labels were only *just* legible, so it was easy to find what you wanted, but still nothing seemed to be on crass display either. On the second shelf were the boxes of creams and bandages, and they were all artfully *arranged* like an intricate puzzle, one piece fitting next to or above the other with no unused space in between. And the third shelf was bare. No stray tube of ChapStick or near-empty bottle of Tums. Just totally, completely, unquestionably bare.

"My God," I breathed, and was, of course, forced to compare this medicine cabinet to the ones in our house, and it was a sorry comparison. Our medicine cabinets, like really most everything else in our house, seemed to be trapped inside a permanent blizzard of disorganization. It was a challenge to find anything ever. When my son did his homework there would first have to be a period in which we searched for a ruler, a pencil sharpener, an assignment given to him a few days before and subsequently misplaced. When one of us got sick, it was a minor miracle if the thermometer could be unearthed before the recovery. Recipes had to be abandoned or modified because I could not find the jar of capers inside the overflowing pantry shelves. Small and large household repairs went undone because the hammer or screwdriver or pliers had mysteriously disappeared from the tool cabinet in the garage. I wasn't even sure where the Neosporin was in our house, let alone the Bactine.

Needless to say, it was a challenge to live the way that we did, but there was something about the makeup of my son, my husband, and myself that made it impossible for us to live any other way. We knew disorganization was wrong, and we would occasionally try to whip our house into shape, but like an unstoppable weed, the messiness would soon reign once again. These were the cards we had been dealt, we would always at some point be forced to admit, and what could we do but play them?

But standing there, staring at the medicine cabinet in Lyle's house that morning, I was suddenly filled with nothing short of awe and couldn't help but wonder *who* had done this? Was it the Chinese mother or the even-tempered, seemingly open-minded father, or both? Was this a project the two did together, the way other couples cook things like bouillabaisse or plan elaborate car trips? Or was it Lyle? Was he one of those Lego-loving kids who could lose themselves inside the challenge of conquering this space (something my son would never do in a zillion years)? Whose hands had placed each bottle of cough syrup at that just-so angle? Who had devised the mosaic of boxes of Benadryl cream and Tecnu anti–poison ivy soap? And how did everything always get put back in its right place?

I don't know how long I stayed in Lyle's bathroom, but it must have been for quite a few minutes, just staring at the inside of his medicine cabinet as if it were an extremely compelling piece of art, one that gave me, I don't know, maybe pleasure, maybe not. It felt a lot like nourishment, but also in the end, as the dog and I walked away from the house, it left me feeling more than a little bit disturbed.

I PLANNED to call Lyle's parents that night and tell them what I had done. It wasn't an exceptionally busy night. I made dinner (veal Milanese with an arugula salad on the side and homemade butterscotch pudding for desert), and while I cooked Max avoided doing his homework by lying on the couch and reading an old *Doonesbury* comic book. My husband, Patrick, came home and started drinking wine and told me about his day. We ate. After dinner, Max avoided doing his homework by taking a long bath, Patrick went down to the basement to play his guitar, and I washed the dishes. By the time Max got out of the bath, he only had about a half hour to do his homework before bedtime, not enough time to get all that he had to do done, and he started to panic and I told him that it drove me absolutely crazy that he was always doing this to himself, and through his tears he told me now he was surely going to fail and was too tired to do anything about it, and I took him in my arms and told him he wasn't going to fail but had better get up early and really do his homework then. The dog mainly slept.

When I went to bed that night I told myself I had forgotten to make the call to Lyle's parents, but that wasn't true. I didn't forget. I just could not bring myself to tell them I had been inside their empty house. It seemed both shameful and also like a stolen gem I now possessed and did not want to give up: the ability to go secretly into their house when no one else was there. If I told them what I had done, they might decide to move the hidden key. If I told them what I had done it might affect the way they felt about my son, and Lyle was Max's best friend. Max needed Lyle. I didn't want to screw that up. What I had done, it was embarrassing when I thought about it in retrospect, yes. But it was also oddly exciting to know I could, if I wanted to, do it again. And, really, I couldn't give that up. That possibility.

I DIDN'T go back for a few days, but then one morning I had taken the dog for an exceptionally long walk and suddenly felt very thirsty. I badly needed a glass of water and realized I was very close to Lyle's house. It wouldn't be that big a deal if I just popped in for a glass of water, I thought. I mean, everyone knows dehydration could, after all, lead to death . . . right?

I tied the dog to the deck railing and did not even bother to knock this time before letting myself in. I felt a little more self-conscious entering the empty house because I wasn't, like the first time, in a mind-altering-fear-of-death panic and considered turning around and leaving, but instead, I just stood there in the quiet empty house and told myself I wouldn't stay long—I was, after all, just going to have a glass of water. A quick little glass of water. And did I feel my throat begin to hurt? Was I experiencing maybe a wee bit of dizziness? I was trying to remember the other signs of acute dehydration when I stepped into their large and airy living room and then did not take another step.

Like all the other rooms in the house, it was painted a neutral white, but there was something about the spare but perfectly chosen furniture arranged upon a richly colored, intricately woven rug that gave it a more formal air. The furniture was not a matched set. Two of the chairs were heavy mission revival pieces with worn and cracked leather seats, and the couch was some kind of modern design in a boomerang shape covered with shiny aquamarine-colored fabric that made it look wet. But it was not the furniture that grabbed my attention. It was, once again, a vision of perfect order, this time in the guise of the bookshelves that lined the walls.

I could not tell you a single title of a single book because it was not *what* I was looking at, but *how* those books were arranged that I found fascinating. Once again, they all fit perfectly. Every book belonged exactly where it had been placed.

All of the large architectural books were on one shelf, arranged by subject (architect). The quality fiction paperbacks were on another shelf in strict alphabetical order (by author). And at the very top was a vast selection of travel books that covered every place in the known world and were arranged in groups defined by their shared continent. *How did they do that*, I began to wonder. *How did they know with such certainty where each book belonged—and then once it was in its perfect place, how did they manage to always put it back there?*

My God, I thought, my heart starting to beat in a noticeable and not particularly pleasant way. Carelessness had truly been conquered in this house. Randomness, I realized with awe and fear and envy, had been banned.

THAT NIGHT when Max was racing around the house, looking for a glue stick so he could finish his poster on the Peloponnesian War that was due the next day, I, who was loading the dishwasher, but still thinking about those damn bookshelves, looked over to my husband, who was refilling his glass with red wine with one hand and petting the top of the dog's head with the other, and asked, "Is this normal?"

"Having a second, or is this my third, glass of wine?" he asked, and then stopped petting the dog to flip through the messy pile of mail that had sat on the far corner of the kitchen table all during dinner, in the exact same place I had dumped it earlier that day.

"No . . . this total and complete lack of order in our house. Do you think it's normal, Pat?"

My husband shrugged and fished a Musician's Friend catalog

out of the pile of mail and turned to the page featuring the current inventory of really big amps.

"I go out every day and bring home the bacon," he said. "This alleged lack of normalcy in the house is, I believe, *your* problem."

I won't tell you how many times I went into Lyle's house because I don't really remember. Let's just leave it at once or twice a week over a period of two or three months. At first I would visit a different room and find something—a dresser drawer or desktop arrangement or the placement of sweaters on top of a closet shelf that would mesmerize me. Then, after I had been in each room, I went back and revisited my favorite spots and was always a little relieved, but also perturbed, to find them virtually unchanged.

I never stayed long. No more than ten minutes, and I didn't touch anything until the day when I was poking around the kitchen cabinets and noticed an interesting box of mint green tea—Moroccan Mint, it was called—and impulsively decided to make myself a cup. The tea was delicious—both sweet and slightly medicinal tasting—and from that time on, I made myself some whenever I visited. Of course, I washed the cup and carefully put it back exactly where I found it, and then, not wanting to leave any evidence even in their trash, I always took the spent tea bag with me. It was still winter, and I was slightly shocked at how quickly the bag changed from being pleasantly warm to lifelessly cold inside the shelter of my cupped, gloveless hand.

I HAVE a good friend who lives on the opposite coast. An unstated but unwavering law of our friendship is that we always show each other complete and unquestioning support. When she called to tell me her husband was leaving her, I told her, "Good riddance! This is the best thing that ever happened to you!" When I called to tell her I was taking my son out of private school and throwing him into the wild, unpredictable seas of the public school system, she told me that was going to be great for him. When she called to say that even though she couldn't afford it, she was going to buy her youngest daughter a pony, I told her, no matter the cost, it would be, in terms of her daughter's development and mental and emotional well-being, totally worth it, and so when I could no longer stand keeping my secret anymore, she was the one I told.

"Oh . . ." she said in the mild, nonjudgmental way I had expected, as if I had just told her about a new type of laundry detergent I had started to use. "And why are you doing this?"

"I don't know," I answered honestly. "It . . . I don't know. Do you think it's wrong?"

"Well . . . I don't know about *wrong* . . ." she continued in her belovedly even way. "But . . . it may not be exactly *legal* . . ."

"I never take anything . . ."

"What about the tea?"

"God . . . you should see the way she keeps her shoes," I said, and the memory brought forth the feelings I had when I was inside the house, ones of awe and jealousy and, the more I visited, a kind of *pride* in what I knew was not mine (really, I did understand that), but somehow it all started to feel like

it belonged to me in a weird way. "They're totally color coor-
dinated . . ."

"Really? Does she have a lot of shoes? Are her feet big?"

"Yes. She has tons of them. And no. They're tiny. The
shoes."

"Small shoes always look so much better than big ones. I'm
worried about you . . ."

"Why? Do you think I'm going crazy?"

"No! No! You're fine . . . but, I don't know. Maybe you
should try, well, doing something."

"What do you mean?"

"I don't know. Maybe get a job. Get out in the world a little
more. You know . . ."

"But I'm not hurting anything," I pleaded. The notion of
getting out into the world a little more did not sit well with
me. "I mean, it's not like I'm hurting anyone . . ."

"Well, you *are* drinking their tea."

"Do you really think I have to?"

"What?"

"Stop going there?"

"Well . . . I don't know . . . I mean, maybe . . . well . . .
yes!"

I LISTENED to my husband snore. Outside, all of the leafless
trees moved as if in slow motion in the late winter wind. The
dog, at the foot of our bed, barked in the muted voice of her
dreams. Downstairs, in a bedroom that is supposed to be for
guests, Max, who never liked the room he was given in this
house, slept.

I wondered what was going on in Lyle's house, a place that

I had come to know so well I could close my eyes and imagine myself there. I wondered if they were all asleep and if they maybe slept better than we did, knowing that everything in their house was in its perfect place. I wondered if their vigilance at keeping order availed them of a peace of mind that I would never know. Downstairs in *my* kitchen, in *my* house, the top of the table was still covered with grains of couscous from dinner. The boxes of all of my books remained stacked in my office, still, after months of living here, not unpacked. The broken front doorbell sat inexplicably on the counter next to the toaster and a remote-controlled fart-sound machine. My son's clothes hung out of his drawers—the pieces that hadn't fallen completely onto the floor. In the corner of our bedroom were stacks of shoes my husband never wore. And that was just a short list of the things that were not as they should have been in my house. That was just the tip of the iceberg. I could have gone on. I could have, I realized in my frozen state of sleeplessness, gone on and on and on.

I TOLD myself that this would be the last time, and maybe I meant it and maybe I didn't, but in the end, it was. The last time. I don't remember if I sensed anything was different when I picked up the key from under the mat, but the minute I stepped inside I felt it. The presence of another, and once sensed, I could do nothing but freeze like the proverbial deer in the headlights. And that was what Lyle saw when he came out of the kitchen, a glass of water in his hand, his friend's mother standing there inexplicably in his house, staring at him with what I would imagine to be an expression of embarrassed surprise.

"Lyle!" I demanded irrationally. "What are you doing here?"

He looked at me in a blank, stunned way, and then just continued to stare, but to my relief, did not ask the obvious question, which was, of course, what was *I* doing inside *his* house, and instead just said in a low, tired voice, "I didn't feel good . . . I needed to come home."

"But-but-but the school . . ." I heard myself start to stutter, what I tended to do when extremely agitated. "Th-th-they can't just send you home to an empty house, can they?"

Lyle continued to look at me from behind his glasses with eyes that seemed dark with knowledge that I had hoped no one would ever have.

"I just left. I didn't feel well," he spoke in a bone-weary way. "I wanted to come home."

I swallowed and tried to get a grip on the situation, and that was when I noticed that the kid actually looked pretty sick. His cheeks were unnaturally flushed, and his body, while still standing, seemed oddly limp. I began to wonder nervously what was wrong with him and how contagious it might be, and really, being around sick people was not one of my strong suits, and what I wanted to do was just turn around and get out of that house, but I knew that I couldn't.

"Well . . . I think you should call your parents," I said, not moving, trying to handle this whole situation from what I hoped was a safe distance. With all of the orderliness in their lives it was quite possible this family had a plan for just this kind of emergency (something that, of course, *we* would never have), like an arrangement with a neighbor or relative close by who could be summoned and quickly release me from this trap I had so stupidly fallen into.

"I'm not going back to school," Lyle mumbled as he wearily stumbled past me and into the den.

"I didn't say that." I turned and watched as he collapsed on the couch and then just lay there with his shoes still on, his head resting heavily on an embroidered pillow I had always admired. "I just said, you should call your parents and tell them that you're here and you're sick."

"They'll make me go back to school. Unless I have a fever I have to go to school . . . That's the rule . . ."

"Do you think you have a fever?" I asked, sounding scared even to my own ears.

"I don't know."

"Well . . . do you feel hot? Do you feel achy? Does your head hurt?"

"Affirmative on all accounts," he mumbled in a foggy way, as if responding to a voice in a dream, and that's when I knew I was really fucked.

WELL, I did what I had to do. I brought the kid some Motrin and a second glass of water. I covered him with the blanket I knew was always neatly folded on the second-to-bottom shelf in the hall closet. I looked up his doctor on a typed list of emergency numbers that I had previously noted was taped to the door of the cupboard filled with everyday glasses. I called the doctor and they told me to take Lyle's temperature, and so I went up to the master bathroom and got the thermometer out of the top right-hand drawer. The whole time I was doing these things it was as if I were on a TV show acting out someone else's life and I felt actually more confident dealing with this crisis than I had ever felt in my own house because, at least, for once I knew with complete certainty where everything I needed would be.

Holding my breath, I put the thermometer into Lyle's mouth and then quickly stepped away. I looked at my watch and then looked back at Lyle and saw he was as still as a statue, inanimate except for the rise and fall of his chest with each seemingly excessively deep and perhaps even labored breath, but his eyes were open and he was looking at me in a curious, perhaps even suspicious way.

I knew what he was thinking, of course. He was wondering what I was doing there. He, who lived in a house where everything had its place, knew I had no place there.

Deciding it would be best to get the explanation out of the way while he still had the thermometer in his mouth and couldn't question me further, I started nervously, "Boy. It was really weird . . . I was just out walking the dog when I looked over and saw someone inside your house . . . I couldn't see who it was, but I could tell it wasn't your mother or father. And I know no one's supposed to be here during the day, right? I mean, I *know* that. So, I decided to get a closer look and remembered Max told me about that key you keep under the mat and thought maybe I better come in and see what was going on."

Lyle mumbled something that I couldn't understand because of the thermometer in his mouth.

"What?" I asked, and Lyle took the thermometer out and repeated his question. "But why didn't you knock first?"

"Oh," I said, my mind racing. "I thought about knocking, but then decided the person who was here might not answer the door. I mean, maybe they were here when they shouldn't've been, right? So, that's why I just let myself in. And boy, wasn't it lucky that I did?"

All at once, Lyle started to cough, a horrible, deep, strangled-animal kind of cough, and I was horrified to note that he did not cover his mouth, either. Acting solely on instincts, I covered my nose and mouth with the cupped palm of my hand and jumped even further away, feeling my heart start to pound in the same way it did when I thought I might have just unwittingly caught it—the disease that was going to do me in, take me down for good, erase me from my world.

"Are you okay?" I asked when Lyle finally stopped coughing, and he nodded weakly before he squinted at the thermometer and announced in a flat voice, "I have a temperature of a hundred and four . . ."

"*What?*" I screamed.

"Well . . . no," he said and squinted harder at the thermometer, and I allowed myself a second of optimism, the thought that he had really meant something more like one hundred *point* four, a common mistake, but all hope was instantly vanquished when he wearily announced the correct reading: "More like a hundred and four and a third . . ."

"Oh . . . well, gee, Lyle . . . You're really sick," I said, feeling nauseous and cold and hot and as if I was going to cry, but trying hard not to show it, and Lyle sighed and closed his eyes again and became once more eerily motionless.

"Okay," I said, as a way to convince myself that what I was doing—taking care of a sick kid—a *very* sick kid for parents who led *very* organized lives in a *very* organized house, but who were still unavailable to deal with this messy situation—was really something I was going to be able to handle. "Okay . . ."

DRIVING TO the doctor's office, I rolled down my window as much as I could stand and tried to keep Lyle talking because when he went silent I got really scared. I asked him about school, playing Little League in the spring, even *The Lord of the Rings*, but he clearly did not want to talk and I noticed when I glanced back at him in the rearview mirror, his complexion had gone from flushed to a frightening pale.

I had left messages on both parents' voicemails, explaining the whole story pretty much the same way I had told it to Lyle—about walking by the house and thinking I had seen someone inside and so had come to investigate and, boy, was it ever lucky that I did because Lyle was really sick and I was taking him to the doctor and asked them to call me on my cell as soon as possible.

I glanced anxiously at the silent phone that sat on the empty front seat beside me and tried to will it to ring. It didn't.

The air coming into the car from the open windows was frigid, and my hands on the steering wheel were growing achingly cold, but my gloves were in the pocket of the coat covering Lyle in the backseat. I thought he might be asleep, and I didn't want to disturb him. I squeezed my fingers into fists, first with one hand off the wheel and then the other, and took turns holding them against the heating vent. I did not want to roll the windows up yet. I wanted fresh air. Gallons of it. A river of it. I turned the heat all the way up and drove slowly across the black, icy roads. I looked back again at Lyle and watched as he shifted restlessly.

"Are you warm enough, dear?" I asked.

"Yes," he answered very quietly.

"We're almost there," I told him.

"Good," he sighed.

"You're going to be fine," I said with probably more hope than certainty, before I absentmindedly put a hand on my own forehead and then just left it there, knowing that it would be a few days before the illness could announce itself, and prayed the tires of the car would keep their grip on this not-at-all-to-be-trusted road.

PREDATION

WHAT WE THINK ABOUT a lot in our house is *extinction*. We think about the extinction of the dinosaurs. We think about the extinction of the ice age animals. We think about the extinction of my friend Larry.

"SAY *CUP*," my son, Hank, shouts from his bedroom where he is looking for a tiny toy saddle. "Say *horse*."

WHAT I have found interesting about parenthood is how bad I am at it. This has come as a surprise. I always pegged myself as a natural and went through years of highly unnatural manipulations and unspeakable anguish to have Hank only to—in my opinion—completely fail in what is probably the most important role of my life.

This is not really surprising, and by *this*, I mean my complete miscalculation of what my true nature would be. That lack of self-awareness could, in fact, be the story of my life, which if it were just me going through this journey by myself would probably be pretty comedic, but throw a kid into the mix and, unfortunately, the dye of comedy quickly changes into something entirely different.

"SAY *ooombabaooomba!*"

IF LARRY were still here, he would shake his head at all this. He was an optimist, sailing past bad tidings as if they were complete strangers, unseeable.

"You have to always look at the bright side, baby doll," he told me when I was pathetically crumpled on the pet groomer's floor, lost in the despair that can only come from another failed romance.

"Bright side?" I repeated incredulously.

"So, you made a mistake. He wasn't the right one for you. Now he's cleared the spot for someone better. In the end this fellow would've been more trouble than he was worth." Larry spoke in a calm and confident voice, carefully putting the blow-dryers (different sizes for different-size dogs) back on their hangers.

"Yeah. Yeah. Yeah," I mumbled, and picked the dog hairs off of the tile closest to me and held them above my head before releasing them so I could watch them float, almost invisible, back to the floor. Larry, who was considerably older than I was and so had certainly seen his share of sadness, never allowed himself to be pulled down by the weight of loss and disappointment. He had what is known as a buoyant personality. Larry was remarkably unsinkable.

"I'm laying my wager on you," Larry said soothingly, and reached out to lightly pet the top of my head as if I were one of his favorite dogs, a special one that he gave extra biscuits to and tied the prettiest ribbons on. "Take it to the bank, Maria. You're going to be fine."

And despite my better judgment, I would try to believe him. What choice did I have? I was a single mother; I had to keep soldiering on. The bed of utter despair was not mine to lie in for long. It was just so good to have Larry there to breathe hope into our lives when I was sure there was none.

So, of course, only the worst could happen to him.

"SAY *bang, bang.*"

"LIFE'S NOT fair," says the voice of Jeremy Irons as Scar, the evil uncle in *The Lion King*, a movie I've seen far too many times for anyone's good, let alone for a four-year-old who, if allowed, would probably watch it every day of his life. This is one of those parenting things that I am truly terrible at: *setting limits.* Actually, I have never been good with any sort of *limits.* I'm claustrophobic, for God's sake. Just the word, *limits*, does something to my lungs, makes it hard for me to breath.

For about a month after Larry was killed, I let my son, Hank, watch *The Lion King*, *Beauty and the Beast*, and *Pocahontas* every day. In my despair, I rationalized that the almost constant rotation of Alan Menken lyrics could be a positive thing—something about how the healing power of overproduced, emotionally manipulative, relentlessly upbeat songs

would get us through this most terrible of terrible times—
and I most probably would still be telling myself this if Hank's
actual (but never present) father, Tag, had not shown up unan-
nounced one foggy Tuesday evening, only to step into the
house and scream, *"Shut that shit off!"*

A word about extinction and how to explain it to a four-
year-old: Well, what you say when you are inside the George
C. Page La Brea Tar Pits Museum, gazing with your silent and
scared son at the growling/howling animated mannequins of a
saber-toothed tiger preparing to plunge its large canines into
the neck of a blank-eyed ground sloth is "They all died off."

"They're dead?" the four-year-old asks in the unnervingly
quiet tone he's adopted since Larry's murder.

"Yes. All of them. For years and years and years," I say as
cheerfully as possible.

"What do you mean, all of them?" he asks, nervously biting
the inside of his cheeks.

"I mean, there's no such thing as saber-tooths or ground
sloths or mastodons or wooly mammoths anymore, darling."

"Do you mean they aren't real?"

"Right. They aren't real."

"So, are they make-believe?"

And if the four-year-old's brown eyes had any magical power
they would command me to nod my head, smile reassuringly,
and give him the teeny-tiny thing he's asking for—the comfort of make-believe, the almost-but-not-quite realness of it.
And I want to give it to him. I want to with all my heart, but
for some reason I can't. No, sir. Not me. Instead, I look away,
lock eyes with that poor, screaming sloth—who is eternally

trapped in that second that is worse than death, the one when you know with absolute certainty you're going to die, and if you have time to hope, you only hope it's not going to be as bad as you know it will be—before I take my child's hand, a small spot of warmth against my bigger, colder palm and say as gently as I can, "No, sweetie, they're not make-believe. They're nothing. Absolutely nothing."

LARRY WAS not a young man when he died. He never told me how old he was but in their accounts of the murder the papers listed his age as sixty-four. Sixty-four is not young, but it's not really old, and if that unknown assailant hadn't come into the store just before closing on that unseasonably warm Monday, my day off, I believe Larry would've been by my side grooming dogs for many more years to come.

He really had a true talent for the work. I was good at nails, but that was more about speed than technique. The other part, the actual grooming, I could do a decent job of if the dog was real old or tranquilized (something I never did without the owner's consent), but Larry just had the natural touch. There was something about the way he whispered to the dogs and stroked their fur that seemed to make them feel instantly safe, certain of being well cared for.

"It's from all my years in show business," he once told me. "Believe me, a rabid Dobie is nothing next to Mitzi Gaynor on a bad night."

"TIME TO get ready for bed," I said, and picked Hank off the floor where he and Tag had been playing an elaborate game with his Fisher-Price toys.

"When will I see you again, Daddy?" Hank asked, delighted as always to see Tag, the man he calls *Daddy* (which is technically correct I guess but still bugs me).

Tag shrugged and said, "How 'bout tomorrow, kiddo?"

"You're coming back tomorrow?" Hank asked excitedly, and smiled first at Tag and then at me. I raised my eyebrows and gave Hank a surprised look and tried to smile in order to hide the fact that this surprise was far from a happy one for me.

"No, man. I ain't leaving," Tag said, and my faint smile instantly vanished, but before I could say a single word, Tag headed out of the room to get himself a beer.

"So, did the fag leave you any money?" Tag asked a little later that night after I had finally gotten Hank to sleep. He finished his beer in one long gulp and then sat down too close to me on the living room sofa. I just gave him a look of utter disgust.

"All right, all right, Maria. Allow me to rephrase the question," Tag said, and moved closer, forcing me to scoot further away. "So, did the *dude*—is that better?—your *friend*, the unfortunate bastard, leave you something?"

"Go!" was all I could bring myself to say. Utterly exhausted, I was no longer able to calculate the number of days that had passed since I had had a good night's sleep. "Just leave, Tag!"

I pointed toward the front door but Tag gently pushed my arm back down and looked at me with his "innocent" face, the same one he wore when he used to stumble into bed at five in the morning, claiming he lost track of time playing gin rummy with his mother.

"I have nowhere to go, Mar. I'm not going back to Melissa. Man, that chick just got too, too, too *emotional*!" Tag shook his head, and I thought Melissa must have started agitating for a commitment, something I could have told her was never going to happen and a bad move to play with Tag. Tag looked at me again and smiled slightly, saying something with his eyes that I both did and did not want to see, or hear.

I quickly stood up and walked across the room and turned off a light and then turned off another.

"What are you doing here, anyway, Tag? Surely, you have other places . . ."

I spoke quietly, because it was almost midnight and Hank had just fallen asleep, but I watched Tag closely, and the weird thing was that in the newly darkened living room, he suddenly looked ten years younger, like he did when we were both in our early thirties and I used to be so in love with him. I wished I had left the lights on.

"Just thought it was time I step up to my parental responsibilities," Tag said. Then he yawned and his forehead crinkled, making him instantly look his age again.

"You're not the parent, Tag. You're the sperm donor. There's a big difference," I was forced to remind him once again.

"Not to me," he said, before stretching out on the couch and firmly closing his eyes.

"Dinosaurs are extinct," Hank explained for about the fortieth time, as I pushed him around Trader Joe's in a shopping cart, a few days before Tag's sudden and unexpected reappearance in our lives. "All of them. The plant-eaters and the meat-eaters."

"I know," I said, and in an effort to change the subject, held up a bag of barbeque potato chips. "Are these the ones you like?"

"That means they're all dead," he continued as if I hadn't said a thing. "The plant-eaters *and* the meat-eaters."

"I know," I sighed, and checked the date on the tortillas—we'd been having a problem with moldy tortillas. "And you know what? The dinosaurs were all dead even before the ice age animals roamed the earth."

"But they're dead too," Hank said, grimly nodding his head.

"Oh, yeah. They are," I agreed.

"They're extinct."

"Right."

"Is Daddy extinct?" Hank asked, his brow now a small crease of confusion.

"No," I sighed.

"Where is he?"

"I don't know." I smiled and shrugged my shoulders to convey the absolutely false message that it's really no big deal not to know the whereabouts of one of your parents. No big deal. Misplaced toy. Misplaced shoe. Misplaced father.

"He could be extinct," Hank offered, helpfully.

"No. I don't think so," I said. "I think he's just busy somewhere else."

"Is Larry busy someplace else?"

"No. Larry's dead. You know that, honey," I said quietly, and lightly ran my fingers over the fine hairs on the top of his head in what I hoped was a comforting way.

"So maybe Daddy's dead," Hank said, and, in my own sick, perverted way, I wanted to give him this point, but I didn't.

"Daddy's not dead, sweetie," I said, and then muttered under my breath as I rummaged in the back of the shelf, hoping to find some fresher tortillas, "I'm just not that lucky."

THE SCENE in Trader Joe's is an example of my failure as a parent. Meaning: Four-year-olds are not supposed to be thinking about death *all the time*. I'm sorry, but they're not. As a parent I should have protected him. I should've guarded my son's innocence with my life. Nothing as piercing as death, *death* we're talking about, should've come within five hundred feet of my child's soul. That night when I'd hung up the phone and Hank had looked at me and asked in a too, too quiet voice what was wrong, I should've said, *nothing*. That's what I should've said. *Nothing is wrong, everything's fine, sweetheart.* But what I said and I wish so much I hadn't was the truth.

BEFORE BECOMING a groomer, Larry had long successful career as a stage manager in Las Vegas.

"When I first got there, it was all Glamour with a capital *G!*" he told me one evening as I cleaned the grooming area, shaking out a thick coat of Clorox over all the white tiles while he counted the day's money. I noticed he often talked about his life in Vegas when he counted money. "I got to work with everyone! Sinatra, Lewis and Martin, Sammy Davis, Ann-Margret, Shecky Greene, Don Rickles, Joey Bishop . . ."

"What about Elvis?" I interrupted, something I knew Larry hated, but I couldn't stop myself. "Did you ever work with Elvis?"

Larry sighed, laid down the stack of tens, and gave me that look of his, the same one I got when I had to ask him to take over a too-jumpy dog: not exactly angry—Larry never got angry—just disappointed.

"Elvis was the beginning of the end," Larry spoke slowly, as if I were slightly mentally retarded. "He attracted a different kind of crowd, if you know what I mean, beauty."

"But did you ever work with him?" I persisted, mainly because I had seen that oddly silent black-and-white footage of Elvis at twenty-one, the black-haired beauty, all fire and nerves, dancing on some outdoor country fair stage, and lost a piece of my heart forever.

"Sweetie, I decided from the beginning never to work on something I didn't care about. There's never any point in doing that!"

I stared down at the dry turquoise powder that was slowly darkening on the damp counter and let him pinch the top of my arm lightly, which was what he did to show affection, all at once feeling so sad because I knew all the work I had ever done I hated, even the grooming—it was just hanging out with Larry that made it tolerable.

"You love doing this, don't you?" I asked.

"What? Talking to you?"

"No, grooming the dogs. You love it, don't you?"

"Honey, I wouldn't be here if I didn't. Because, believe me, life's too short, and Lord knows, I don't need the money!"

IN THE middle of the night, the bedroom door opened and Tag came in and sat down on the edge of the bed.

"Are you sleeping, Maria?" he whispered, and although I considered not answering, I somehow heard myself say, "No."

Tag lay down beside me in the dark. "You need a new couch."

"I know," I said, and turned on my side so my back was facing him. Since I hadn't been sleeping much anyway, I was secretly glad for the company during the long, quiet no-man's hour, even if the company was Tag.

"So, come on, just tell me, what's the money situation like around here these days?" Tag asked.

I didn't answer for a long time. It was a complicated question coming from Tag. A talented but lazy guitarist, he usually earned what money he had by being the lowest of middle men in tiny pot deals, but those deals tended to go bad, and I was worried he was going to ask to borrow some money, something I had specifically promised my parents I wouldn't do when they lent me the ten grand.

"I mean," he said, after a while, "if you need a hundred bucks . . ."

"No, that's okay," I said, quickly. "Dot and Herb actually came through this time."

"Well, stop the world," Tag said with true amazement. That had been a huge point of contention when we were together so many years ago. It drove him nuts that my rich parents would never spread the wealth my way. "They believe in survival of the fittest," I used to explain. "They're trying to make me fit."

"So, how is he?" Tag asked, shifting around beside me on the bed, rearranging pillows under his head.

"My dad?"

"No. The kid."

"I don't know. Not so good, I guess."

"He'll be all right."

"How do you know that?"

Tag thought for a minute. I could feel his breath lightly blowing the hairs on the back of my neck and the heat of his body filling up the small space between us under the covers.

"I guess I don't," he finally admitted, before his hand landed softly on the inside of my thigh, in the exact place I was hoping it would.

I OFTEN dream about Larry and in my dreams he is always happy but never says a word. It's not that he can't speak, but rather he doesn't want to. What he is usually doing is pushing my son on the swing at the park. In real life, Hank is a tireless swinger and Larry used to be a tireless pusher. Sometimes I would fall asleep on the grass under a tree watching them, and those were the sweetest rests of my life.

About a week after the murder, I finally got the nerve up to go back to the store. It was eerie walking into the place, mainly because it was almost exactly the way it was the last time I was there, the stacks of forty-pound bags of Science Diet in the corner, the shelves of neatly lined bottles of Mycodex flea shampoo, and the stubborn smell of wet dog hair still heavy in the air. All the same except for the two bloodstains, one on the white linoleum floor and the second on the far wall, directly behind the cash register.

I stood there for the longest time, unable to look away from the blood. Larry's blood. His blood. Something thick gathered in my throat making it increasingly hard for me to breath, and even though it wasn't what I intended to do, I suddenly found myself filling a plastic bucket with warm tap water.

I started to scrub. I scrubbed and scrubbed and scrubbed. In case you have never done this, the interesting thing that happens is the dried blood that is brown actually turns red again when rehydrated, a bright, beautiful, shimmering red. And when I was done, when the wall was spotless and the tile floor gleaming white, I looked at the water in the bucket that was a gorgeous winelike color—so rich and delicious looking I knew I couldn't pour it down the drain. Instead, I carefully dipped my hands into the sweet-smelling mixture of water, cleansing solution, and Larry's blood and whispered a lot of words, most that probably made little or no sense, before turning and walking, dripping red, out of the store.

"ARE YOU a plant-eater or a meat-eater?" I woke up early and heard Hank ask Tag this. I could feel Hank's small, perfect body wiggling beside me. He had wormed under the covers between me and his father, making the bed feel almost swampy with the three of us in it together.

"I eat both," Tag answered sleepily, and I opened my eyes to see Tag's heavily tattooed arm lazily snake around the child and pull him closer.

"That means you're an omnivore," Hank explained. "I'm an omnivore too. Mommy's an herbivore. She doesn't eat meat."

"Since when?" Tag asked, surprised, knowing my partiality towards rare, red meat.

"Since Larry died."

"It's a Hindi thing," I said, and both Hank and Tag looked at me, surprised I was there. "It's a way of honoring the dead."

"Larry's extinct," Hank said to Tag. "A bad man shot him in the head with his gun. The police didn't catch him. The bad man."

Tag looked at me with not a slight amount of disgust. "Do you two always start the day talking about this shit?"

"Yes," Hank answered before I could lie.

THE THEORIES are (1) a giant meteorite crashed into the earth, releasing poisonous gases and covering the land with an impenetrable cloud of dust that blocked the sun for years and years and killed off all of the dinosaurs; (2) man became a more sophisticated hunter and killed off all of the ice age plant-eating animals, leaving the meat-eating animals nothing to feed on, thus throwing off the balance of the ecosystem and causing all the large animals eventually to die off; (3) a high-on-crack, most probably gang member attempted to rob Larry, got scared, and shot him in the head before running out into the dark street, never to appear again—except in my child's nightmares, where he has landed himself an almost nightly starring role.

I LOVE to stand on the observation platform and watch the gas bubbles explode through the thin sheet of water that covers the largest and most spectacular pit. The air smells deliciously like tar, although we've been told it isn't tar at all, but actually asphalt. On one side of the pit, a steady stream of traffic on Wilshire Boulevard heedlessly passes the statues of the mastodon family, the mother and child who stand on the bank with their trunks raised toward the father who has waded a couple of yards from shore and gotten inextricably stuck.

"Bad luck for him," Hank always says when we see it.

From where I stand, I watch Hank and Tag walk along one of the paths that winds through Rancho La Brea toward a *paleta* man. They are not holding hands but walk side by side, close enough to do so if they wanted to. I notice they have the same bouncy walk.

When I decided I wanted to have a child, I asked Tag to be my sperm donor even though we had been broken up for years. My logic in choosing him was that he was the one man I had ever been with who told me he loved me, and I thought even a technologically produced child should come out of love, even one that is no more.

And Tag really does have his winning side. When I asked him the other day what Elvis was singing in that silent piece of black-and-white film, he didn't hesitate. "Oh! You mean the one shot at the Alabama State Fair in 1956? Oh, it was 'Hound Dog.' You can tell by the way he's moving. It's definitely 'Hound Dog'!"

For the whole week he has been with us, Tag has been on his very best behavior. He washes all of the dishes. Goes out to his car to smoke dope. Reads Hank the endless Richard Scarry books that I long ago deemed too boring and has introduced the kid to T. Rex and Big Mama Thornton. And I can see a lightness returning to Hank's eyes. Just for moments, long moments when the grips of fear seem to loosen their hold and he can once again enter that almost weightless place of being a four-year-old, as light as a comic strip bubble without a word of dialogue inside.

There's a part of me that likes this, but then there's another part that thinks, *here I go again*. What *that* part thinks I really should do is try to keep Hank from getting too attached to this man—I guess, his father—because I know he will desert him. Tag said he loved me and I believe he *did* love me and he left. Tag may not even want to, but that's just who Tag is: a deserter. But days have gone by and I say and do nothing and I can't help but wonder why. Larry would, of course, know the answer. He would know what it is that makes us close our eyes to those things we just cannot face, the giant meteorite hurtling wildly through the cosmos, the bullet coming straight for our heads. Larry would know what it was that kept the mother and child mastodon planted on the edge of the tar pit, calling to the father to come back, please come back, as he sinks helplessly deeper into the thick, hot blackness below. Larry would know—but obviously, he's no longer talking.

DEATH AND DISASTER

'VE ALMOST COMPLETED THE epic task of washing every single dish in the house, when the phone rings. I know it's my mother.

"I have a story for you," she, as always, launches right in. I sigh, cradle the phone against my shoulder, and continue with the dishes. Since my husband, Stephen, left me a few weeks ago, my mother has been calling almost every day to tell me a new tale of woe. The point of these stories is to put my currently fucked-up situation into some kind of new perspective that will make me realize how lucky I actually am because others have it so much worse. I call these stories "My Mother's Death and Disaster Series."

"You know Hilda Cook, Carol Lamar's cousin?" she asks, but doesn't wait for an answer, which is probably good because I have no idea who she is talking about and really don't care.

"Well, Hilda's son-in-law. You remember him? The underemployed actor who has been doing a lot of industrials for Lockheed and Nabisco—"

"Most actors are underemployed," I say, and hold the glass I've just finished washing up to the window to see if I've missed any scum, or more accurately, any of what might be Stephen's residual scum that I am attempting to scrub out of my life.

"Well, Brian and his wife, Hilda's daughter . . . You know they live not too far from you in Echo Park. One of the *nicer* areas of Echo Park, and they have two kids. A girl, six, and a boy, two . . . just two . . ." My mother's voice trails off, and that is when I know that something pretty darn bad has happened to the underemployed actor.

"Mom," I say, because really the accumulative effect of these stories is starting to weigh on me, and I do believe you can court bad tidings by having too many negative thoughts, and the last thing in the world I want is to invite any more bad luck into my life. "I should get going here . . ."

"Wait, wait, let me just finish this," she, as I expected, insists. "So, it seems this Brian was quite the man of the neighborhood, the unofficial Lone Ranger of Echo Park. Head of the Neighborhood Watch and that sort of thing."

"Mom, really, I . . ." I start, but am distracted by the appearance of a strange woman on my neighbors' deck. I see her first through the glass I am holding up to the window, so she appears distorted, her head tiny, body immense, but when I lower the glass I see the distortion was only slight, that the proportions were basically true.

"So, one of his neighbors, an elderly woman, complained to

Brian that another neighbor was parking his car on her front lawn. Can you believe someone would do such a thing? Even in Echo Park? Well, apparently it happens."

I step away from my kitchen window so the woman on my neighbors' back porch cannot see me, but I can still see her. She has very short blond hair, bluntly cut around her small head, and wears an enormous pair of red-rimmed glasses. She looks like an oversize child, weirdly innocent. I am certain I have never seen her before.

"Well, yesterday morning, Brian had a word with the young man who was parking his car on the woman's front yard, and although no one knows exactly what happened because, unfortunately, there were no eye witnesses, apparently Brian and this young man got into quite an argument, and the young man reached inside his car, got a gun, and shot poor Brian in the throat."

"Oh my God," I gasp, and instinctively reach up and touch my own suddenly very vulnerable-feeling neck. "That's terrible, Mom!"

"I know. But wait! It gets worse! He died in the ambulance on the way to the hospital," my mother finishes her tale using an appropriately solemn tone. "The daughter is only six, and the boy, two . . ."

"You're right," I say, and have to blink back tears that have suddenly sprung to my eyes even though I have no idea who this Brian is, but it just seems like all there is, is tragedy in this world, and then even more tragedy, and those whom all of this tragedy befalls are the innocent, the ones trying to do good. I hate my mother for telling me this story, but I hate myself more for listening to it. "That *is* even worse."

After I hang up, I go back to the sink to finish the dishes and see the woman is still there on my neighbors' porch. *Who is she*, I wonder again. *Why is she there? What does she want?* Then she suddenly smiles and I think she must have spotted me. She lifts one of her hands and I am just about to wave back, when I see a small green parrot glide down from the sky and land gracefully on the tip of the woman's outstretched fingers. Slowly and gently, the strange woman brings the bird up to her compact face and plants a kiss on its hard, sharp beak. Then, with a small, secret grin, she turns and heads inside my neighbors' house, and I think I hear the parrot say in a kind of raspy voice, "Time's on my side," before the door closes behind them.

I HAVE ESP or something like that. I can predict things like the next song the DJ's going to play on the radio, or describe the layout of furniture in rooms I have not been in yet when I go into a stranger's house, and tell them about pets they had when they were children.

Stephen and I were always trying to cash in on these skills.

"I mean, can't you like hone it so you can sniff out truffles or something like that?" Stephen would wonder in the middle of the night when we were lying there, sleepless, worrying about money.

For most of our time together, Stephen was a freelance journalist and I, a professional temp. We were both good at what we did, but unfortunately neither of us made much money. This seemed fine when we first got together, but living in a small one-bedroom bungalow in what my mother has always referred to as the not-*yet*-nice area of Silver Lake and driving old, barely-running cars and never being able to go on great vacations like our friends with real jobs began to get old.

The thing is I'm pretty sure if I wanted one I could have a career. I'm such a great temp I'm often asked to stay on in a permanent position, one with real benefits and a clear upward trajectory, but invariably, I decline. I do this because the one thing I know about myself is if I make anything permanent, I mean for seriously real, I am destined to fuck it up.

It was for this very reason I put off getting married. I knew once Stephen and I made it official, our relationship would go exactly where it went—straight to hell. We were together seven years, and for six of them I resisted getting married even though I loved Stephen more than I thought it possible to love another person. I loved the way he looked. I loved the way he smelled. I loved the way his voice sounded and almost every word he said. Just being with him made me feel more like myself but better, the person I had always wanted to be. And he, I suppose, for his own reasons, also loved me.

"Marry me, Cin," I'd wake up in the morning and hear him whisper into my ear. "Marry me," he'd mumble from within his pillows before he fell asleep. "MARRY ME!" he'd scream across a busy street when he came to rescue me after another Toyota breakdown. "*Marry me, marry me, marry me,*" he used to sing in the shower after we made love.

But I wouldn't. I couldn't. I didn't want to ruin what we had. Then Stephen gave me the ultimatum, "Marry me or I'm leaving," and so I did. I did it because the truth was I would do anything not to lose Stephen, even something that I knew in the end would make me lose him.

I AM putting the last of the clean dinner plates away when the doorbell rings and I know without looking it is the woman I saw earlier on my neighbors' porch.

I open the front door and the woman immediately hands me a plate of brownies. I notice they are covered with so many layers of cellophane that they look unreal, like the wax food they make in a small factory on the edge of Little Tokyo, where I temped once. I remember it being a pleasant place to work. I just had to answer a phone that barely ever rang, so I had plenty of time to watch the workers carefully fold green sheets of wax into individual lettuce cups and pour the hot golden-colored wax into the tempura shrimp molds.

Up close, the woman looks less childish. She is probably around my age, in her early thirties, yet there is a definite air of innocence around her, as if she hasn't yet developed the proper thickness of skin that would protect her from all of life's uncertainties.

"Hi?" I say, friendly, but also curious. She does not say anything and instead begins to write on one of those pads that kids use. I think they are called magic slates.

You don't know me, I read over her shoulder as she prints in large, childish script, hastily filling the whole pad with those four words.

"Yes," I agree, and then watch as she lifts up the plastic part of the slate and with a very satisfying ripping sound her words disappear.

I'm Libby, she writes. *I can hear, but not speak.*

Even though she has just told me that she can hear, I inexplicably fall silent and just nod my head. For the second time that day my fingers inadvertently reach up and touch my throat.

An image comes into my brain. It is sudden and violent, two hands grasping hold of a neck and squeezing tight. My heart pounds and I am relieved when Libby lifts the plastic sheet and those words vanish.

I'm Michael's sister, she writes and for a second I can't remember who Michael is, and then I do. Michael is my neighbor Wayne's new boyfriend. Wayne brought him by a few months ago and introduced him to Stephen.

"Stephen," Wayne had said. "This is Michael. He's my lover."

Stephen had blushed and looked at his shoes as he politely shook Michael's hand.

Because this is the first time I've ever had a "conversation" with a mute, I'm not really sure what I'm expected to do. So once again, I just nod.

I'm staying at their house for two weeks while they're in Alaska, Libby writes in a script small enough to get all of those words on the pad, and I think, *Alaska? What the heck are those two wild party boys doing in Alaska?* but decide that would probably demand too long of an answer and so don't ask.

Wayne made these for me, Libby writes and nods at the plate of brownies I continue to hold. *But I want to lose ten pounds, so I*

I wait, but Libby does not write anything else and I realize with a start that it's my turn to pick up the conversation.

"Oh, well, thanks," I say, suddenly feeling shy. There is something about this woman that makes me want to protect her, but from what? From what? "They look delicious. I'm sure they are delicious. Everything Wayne makes is just yummy!"

Oh, God. A flush of anger and embarrassment immediately spreads over me. I would never have said a word like *yummy*

if Stephen was still here. The better person I was when I was
with him would never say something stupid like that.

I glance up, expecting to see scorn in Libby's eyes, but what
I see through the thick lenses of her glasses is only a kind of
wordless curiosity, but about what, I am not sure.

"Well, um . . . would you like to come in?" I ask, and am
immediately sorry, but once I've made the offer, I feel like I've
got to try to make it at least sound sincere. "I could make us
some tea, or even coffee? I drink tea. My husband, or rather
my ex-husband, was the coffee drinker, and I think he may
have left some here. Do you want me to check?"

There is a pause as if Libby were reading my words as well
as listening to them. Then she mildly shakes her head no. I
give her a second to write some kind of polite and most probably insincere refusal, but she doesn't.

"Well," I say, and can't quite hide my relief that our interaction is almost over. "Thanks, again."

Libby, of course, says nothing but she looks searchingly into
my eyes and it feels as if she is making a deal with me, a silent
one that I do not quite understand. I wait for some clarifica-
tion, another messily scrawled message on her magic slate,
but she doesn't do that, and instead I watch her shoulders
slump as she turns and starts to walk away.

"Libby!" I call just when she reaches the end of my walk-
way. I know our conversation has somehow disappointed her
and I want to give it at least one more try. But when she turns
and looks back at me with what seems like hope, I don't know
what to say.

"My name's Cindy," I try, and immediately sense this isn't
what she wanted from me either and try one more thing. "If

you need anything, I'm here. I mean, this is where I live . . . alone."

Libby, once again, has no response. She holds the magic slate with the last words she wrote still clear and black against her chest, and I feel the last word I spoke, *alone*, sticking to me. It is like a dull ache, one I cannot seem to lose.

I NEVER liked the idea of the book Stephen set out to write, *From Donner to Dahmer: Annals of Cannibalism in America*, but I wonder now how hard it would have been to feign a little enthusiasm and interest when he told me things like, "Ed Gein used to hang some of his female victims right next to the pigs in the smokehouse to give the flesh a kind of hickory flavor"? But I couldn't do it. I just could not and instead would look away, put my hands over my ears, and hum loudly, hoping to drive the horrible image away before my brain could truly embrace it.

This did not work. I know because at unexpected moments I will suddenly picture four noses resting inside a cereal bowl, or a pair of human lips dangling from a string, or a woman's heart glistening in a cast-iron frying pan.

Having these images floating around in my head is pretty bad, but what's really disturbing is that these images come to me more easily and frequently than a single memory of the happy times Stephen and I shared. These horror-movie stills are clearer and more focused than any of my real memories of real times. Somehow, against my will, they have become a part of me.

I am wondering how this could've happened, how I allowed it to happen, as I stuff some T-shirts Stephen accidentally left behind into the drum of the Weber. I thoroughly drench the cloth with lighter fluid and then set it ablaze. The flames are instant and impressive. I stand back slightly and stare, hypnotized, at the smoke as it gathers, thick, black, and noxious and think about Stephen's accusations that I did not support him writing this book, not because I found the subject matter disgusting and objectionable, but because I was trying to keep him from moving forward in this world. I wonder if there was any truth to this. Was I afraid of either of us moving forward in life? Did I secretly want to keep time at a standstill? And if so, why? I stare harder into the smoke, waiting for the answers to these questions to come to me, but instead I hear a weak but actually pretty accurate imitation of Bob Weir singing, "Livin' on reds, vitamin C, and cocaine."

I look up and see Libby's parrot circling directly above my head. I glance over at Michael and Wayne's yard to see if Libby is once again standing on the back porch, perhaps watching us with a benign, even amused expression, reassuring me that this isn't as ominous an occurrence as I sense it might be, but Libby is not there.

"Truckin' like the doodah man," the bird surprises me by singing another line of the song. I didn't know parrots could do that. I thought it was just random, the things they say. I notice he is flying in an even tighter circle, flitting in and out of the smoke, just barely avoiding being singed by the tiny pieces of burning fabric that float skyward.

"Go away," I order the bird. "Shoo!"

But the bird does not leave and instead begins to circle lower and even tighter. I can now feel a slight breeze each time he passes my face. I move a few steps to one side, but like a swarm of gnats, the bird moves with me. I try going the other way, but he's still there. Finally, I just duck down and cover my head and hope he will fly away. Irrationally, I blame this on Stephen. Without a career or any clear direction in my life, I would sometimes wonder, *why exactly am I here? Why was I choosing to stay alive?* Then I would just sit quietly for less than a second, and the same answer would always come to me: *Stephen. Stephen is my reason for being.* Since he left, I've felt unusually vulnerable to strange and terrible occurrences.

"Truckin', I'm a going home . . . Whoa, whoa, baby back where I . . ." the bird sings as if taunting me. My command for it to leave goes unheeded, and before I know what I'm doing, my arm suddenly flails up over my head, and without looking, I feel my hand hit the bird. It actually hits it quite hard. My palm starts to sting and the bird goes silent. I stay exactly where I am, hunched down beside the barbeque. I do not need to open my eyes to know that the small green body is lying in the center of the crackling fire, my blind aim, of course, perfect.

THERE ARE probably many things Libby can do to me in retribution, I think, nibbling on a brownie. I am sitting in the dark, secretly keeping watch on my neighbors' empty house, well aware I have murdered a mute girl's talking bird. She could slash my tires. She could throw a smoke bomb through my window late at night. She could shoot me in the throat.

I finish one brownie and immediately start another. It is a still night, but I can see the note I taped to my neighbors' door lift and fall in whatever breeze there is. All I wrote was *Libby, come see me. I have something to tell you. Cindy (next door.)*

When I told our neighbor, Wayne, that Stephen had left me for a young librarian at the UCLA research library who had taken a special interest in his project and even helped him get access to material not normally available to nonacademics, he had said nothing, but later, he left a plate of chocolate-chip cookies on my porch with a note that said, *Thought there might be a dearth of sweetness in your life.*

I wonder if Wayne left the same note for Libby with the brownies. I wonder if she came to L.A. not only to lose ten pounds, but also to sweat out some recent bitterness in her life. It seems a little too likely.

The phone rings and since I know it is my mother I do not answer it. After the fourth ring the phone goes silent. My mother has no patience. I sigh and put another brownie into my mouth.

The charred parrot rests on my dining room table wrapped in a piece of yesterday's newspaper. I was surprised how light the bird felt when I fished its hot and stiff body out of the ashes. It was like a piece of mesquite firewood, close to, but not quite, weightless.

Then I get a strange feeling in the pit of my stomach and even before she appears I know Libby has returned. Next, I hear her. She is whistling and she is a beautiful whistler, able to hit every note, her tone rich and resonant. The song is an old Western tune that I recognize, but I do not know the name.

Finally, I see her. She is walking up my neighbors' path toward their front door and her stride is so peaceful it is as if the beauty of her own whistled song is carrying her along. I wonder what she is imagining at this moment, to achieve such a sound. And then I think maybe she is imagining nothing, maybe actually nothing is going on inside her tiny head, maybe she is free from thought, free from memory—real or imagined—and the music, the sad, wistful cowboy tune is just coming straight from the center of her large voiceless body, propelled by nothing, absolutely nothing.

I try to determine if she looks different now that she is a person to whom I have done something terrible, something that will unquestionably cause her pain. But she looks the same. It is the way I see myself, I sadly realize as the brownie inside my mouth turns tasteless like mud, that has, of course, changed.

When Stephen and I first got together and I told him about my so-called psychic abilities, he asked me to close my eyes and tell him what our future was going to be like. I closed my eyes and then said, "Together we will be like Vikings. Together we will discover continents."

When I opened my eyes, Stephen leaned over and kissed me.

That was what I had said, but obviously that was a lie. Now after all those years, I can tell you what I saw that day behind closed eyes when I tried to imagine the future was only what most people see behind closed eyes: blackness, just plain ordinary blackness as thick as smoke, as impenetrable as an old cast-iron frying pan, one large enough to hold the heaviest of human hearts.

NIGHT AND DAY

BAXTER IS CRYING ON the phone. He is a new client and very young, not yet twenty, so I am being patient. It is one in the morning and I stare out the bedroom window at the dark surf, mainly black with rising lines of ghostly white.

"Jewel's left me," Baxter somehow manages to cough out between sobs.

"That's terrible, baby," I say, and since my light is now on, check the bedside BlackBerry to see what's lined up for the next day—well, technically that day, Saturday. It's pretty open until a late afternoon barbeque at a studio exec's house, a concert with a casting agent, and then a party at the home of a not-so-important-at-the-moment-but-could-become-big producer.

"I mean, like . . . like . . . like . . . she's really gone . . ." Baxter says with that pathetic sincerity common to so many of the newly signed—the beautiful young men whose acting careers I manage. "She even took the panda, man."

"What panda?" I toss the BlackBerry back on the nighttable and pick up the mirror to see if I'd been sleeping weird.

"The black-and-white one."

"All pandas are black and white, darling," I say, and am relieved to see my cheeks are crease free and eyes not too hideously puffy.

"Ling-Ling. Jewel always sleeps with Ling-Ling . . . That's like, how I know she isn't coming back . . ."

"Got it," I say, and think these kids are so much younger than I remember being when I was their age. What the fuck did their parents do to retard this generation's emotional development so uniformly?

"What should I do, Peg? I mean, like, really, I think I love her . . . What should I do?" Baxter asks, and the sweet thing is he really wants to know. He wants *me* to tell him.

I shake my head and say quietly, "Why don't you just come over, baby?"

He hesitates and in that hesitation I find myself reconsidering. Although he is a stunning young man, sometimes, at my age, forty-one, a good night's sleep is more tempting than sex and I am just about to retract the invitation when he says softly, like an obedient child, "Okay."

CHECKING THE refrigerator, I see there are still a couple of bottles of root beer, Baxter's drink of choice. If Leon only knew, I think, he would be utterly disgusted. Even seven years ago, he used to bemoan the fact that "the boys" just didn't know how to have a good time anymore.

"Ecstasy! Raves! Snowboarding!" he would shout. "Give me a good old-fashioned revolutionary, any day!"

"Yes, but there is no revolution at the minute, Leon," I would be forced to remind him.

"Oh, Louie," he'd say wistfully, and drape his arm around my shoulder, and because it was Leon, it always felt sexy because everything he did was sexy. "The boys I used to meet at People's Park, you would not believe . . ."

I was twenty-two, just out of college when I was sent by a temp agency to work for Leon, one of the biggest personal managers in Hollywood, and I remember thinking I couldn't be luckier. I mean, Leon was gorgeous, funny, smart, and gay, so basically it was safe to ask him things I felt every young woman starting a career in Hollywood needed to know, like how do you make a studio executive return your phone calls, and what exactly constitutes a *good* blow job. I don't know if he was as immediately taken with me, but after I worked for him a few days and it was revealed I had been a history major at Barnard and written my thesis on the Chinese Revolution, he decided to keep me on as a permanent employee.

"Louie," he nicknamed me, in a nod to *Casablanca*, "this could be the beginning of a beautiful friendship."

CONSIDERING HIS heartbroken state, it doesn't take me long to get Baxter in the sack, or rather for him to think he got me in the sack. That's the game: I pretend to be seduced while, all along, I'm doing the seducing. It works, what can I tell you? Baxter is a beautiful boy as, I guess, they all are. Blond, tall, with a perfect, hairless body—your ideal SS candidate, the one Hitler would definitely have thrown into that mass-producing Aryan babies program. When I kiss him I can still taste the blandness of his boyhood spent in Kansas or Ohio or some other flat state that conjures images of corn dogs, white church steeples, and weekends of heart-stopping boredom.

"Think of it as part of your overall benefits package," Leon said when I doubted the ethical correctness of our almost-routine practice of sleeping with the clients. "And it's a hell of a lot more fun than full dental."

Still, sometimes I feel funny doing what I am doing in what was once Leon's bed, in what was once Leon's house, every-thing almost exactly the way he left it seven years ago, furni-ture, sheets, towels, art—except I took down all the pictures of Leon and put them in milk crates that are in storage in my sister's garage in Culver City. And it's not like I think he would mind me sleeping with the boys in his bed—quite the opposite really—but it's more like I sometimes worry I can't live up to the achievements of the bed's previous occupant, that I am not, nor ever will be, as good as Leon was rumored to be in everything, business, sex, everything, even death.

"You're amazing," Baxter whispers as he hugs me close from behind in a postcoital cuddle.

"No, sweetie, you're the amazing one," I say because, mainly, it is my job to say shit like that.

"Yeah?" he asks so shyly that if I still had a heart, it might actually crumble, but instead, I turn over and lightly kiss the top of his head like you would to comfort a scared child in the middle of the night.

"Oh, totally," I say and sigh. "Totally."

Baxter relaxes in my arms and I can tell he is almost asleep when I ask in a studied casual way, "By the way. You never called. How'd that audition go today?"

"Huh?" he blinks and stiffens slightly.

"The one at Fox," I say in a still relatively nice but focused way. "The comedy the Zankermans are producing."

"Oh . . . yeah . . . that one. They said I was . . . good," he mumbles, and I know he is lying.

"Oh, really?" I say, because when they're new and young, that's all I have to say. They still fear me on a certain level and won't try to pass the untrue off, which I've noticed these young actors do routinely after they've been around the proverbial block.

"Well . . . you know what, actually?" Baxter curls his legs up to his chin in a fetal position. "I kind of, like, missed it."

"You kind of, like, *missed* it?" I repeat.

"Yeah . . . well, Jewel wanted to go ice skating so . . ." His voice trails off to nothingness, into the world of all guilty little boys.

"Not good, Baxter," I say very quietly. "We can't start missing interviews. Do you know how fast that kind of reputation gets around? Pretty, pretty fast. And at this point, they're doing us a favor by seeing you. Until they need you, sweetheart, *nobody* in this town needs you."

To demonstrate how disappointed I am, I slowly roll out of bed and wrap a robe, Leon's old silk robe to be precise, around myself. I step over to the French doors and stare past the deck at the dark restless water. I have lived here so long that I don't even smell the energizing scent of the sea and all of its hidden life or hear the constant but varied beat of the surf anymore. To take notice, I have to make a concerted effort, and I wonder vaguely, *what else have I stopped noticing?*

"Oh, Peggy, don't be mad," Baxter practically whines as he jumps out of bed. I turn away from the dark ocean and just stare at the kid who stands completely naked, so young I can almost smell the newness of the muscles that have appeared on his little boy frame. Slowly, his arms open like a bird preparing for flight or a martyr about to be hammered, pathetically offering up the only things he has that are of any value to me—his beauty, his youth, his promise—in penance.

"Please," he whispers, and I, standing in the darkness, the cool silk of Leon's faded black robe brushing against my body, covering what I know is no longer anyone's standard of perfection, cross my arms and do what Leon taught me to maintain the power—because that is all we have: a kind of power over these kids, these boys, these beautiful specimens that I'm hoping will make me rich, or, more truthfully, richer.

"Keep 'em guessing," Leon used to say. "Never ever give your hand away, Louie . . ."

WHEN LEON took me firmly under his wing and made me a partner in the management firm, he said, "Congratulations. Too bad, one day you're going to hate me for this."

"I'll never hate you," I said, but he had just smiled knowingly and shook his head before picking up a gay S&M magazine and going into his office and closing the door. That was exactly the kind of thing he always did when he sensed I might be on the verge of declaring my love, which I actually managed to do a couple of times, and each time I told him I loved him, Leon responded in the exact same way.

"I know," he would say with both sadness and annoyance.

TAKING A small sip of champagne, I recline on one of the deck's lounge chairs and stare out into the horizon, trying to catch the first signs of daylight, an almost imperceptible brightening, the gradual appearance of details. Even though this is the West Coast, the house is built on some kind of curve, so the sun rises over the water and sets behind my back. Baxter is snoring in the bedroom and I can smell his scent on my skin. It is pleasant and I am not eager to wash it off, although I soon will. That is what I do. Once they leave, I go into the ocean for a quick dip. Even in winter.

One of the things that has changed as I get older is I no longer like to sleep with the boys—I mean, really sleep. I find it disorienting, a feeling akin to seasickness, to wake up beside someone whose name I sometimes cannot remember. When I was younger I used to think that lapse of memory was funny, almost empowering, but that was when I still had Leon to laugh about it with.

What is funny—not ha-ha funny, the other kind—is that once clients leave me for another manager, I can suddenly remember everything about them. My dreams are over-populated with gorgeous young men whose fingers have not touched my skin in years. I taste their sweat, watch their nipples pucker, listen to a chorus of hoarse cries of ecstasy, and wake up filled with longing for those boys I never really had even when they were so briefly mine.

"Easy come, easy go," Leon used to say when a client left

us, and as with most things, he was right. Some of the boys left because they thought they were too big, and some left because they never took off, and some because they lost interest in playing the game and wanted to do something else with their lives. I remember all of them, but the boys who gave the finger to Hollywood are the only ones I respect.

What Leon lost in the year or so before he died was any belief he'd ever had in success. It just became clear to him that the goal, the finish line we were forever racing the clients toward, was just one big Xanadu, a never-to-be-completed monument to actual fulfillment. That was when he started to talk a lot about his ex-radical days in Berkeley and wanting me to tell him about Mao's Long March and the miraculous defeat of the KMT, and only when I told him these stories would his eyes light up again in the same way they used to when he got to negotiate a seven-figure deal.

"Vietnam," Leon said one day, out of the blue. I was sitting on the black leather sofa in his office, supposedly reading the trades, but really daydreaming about one of the boys, Jock Kent, the star of a nighttime soap about a kind of Club Med–like resort where, of course, everyone sleeps with everyone before, both figuratively and literally, stabbing them in the back.

"Is Oliver Stone casting?" I asked, forcing myself to shove away the fantasy (in which, if you must know, Jock and I were having incredible sex in the Hollywood Bowl fountain.)

"You want to go, Louie?" Leon asked, and looked at me in a way that instantly made me uncomfortable.

"Vietnam?" I replied, truly startled, because although I hung out with Leon a lot at his house, he never, *never* asked me to go anywhere with him. I was the one always asking him to go places with me, to screenings, dinners at producers' homes, clients' birthday parties at bowling alleys, invitations that he invariably refused, saying, "Oh Jesus! Don't we see more than enough of each other, Louie?"

"What's in Vietnam?" I asked, suspiciously, and wondered if he was trying to use me to lure some actor (straight) to our agency, a task I had performed gladly when I first started the job, but no longer felt so glad to do.

"Amazing architecture, delicious food, deserted beaches, unspoiled boys . . ." The words came out hard and fast from Leon's mouth like handfuls of pennies thrown onto a sidewalk. There was definitely a desperate quality to his speech, a quality that was absolutely verboten in our line of work where the golden rule is to never act like you want anything, because it'll all but guarantee that you won't get it.

"Yeah. And about a billion tons of bad karma," I said, still convinced there was some underlying motive for this invitation, anxious to put the whole idea to rest.

"What?"

"Leon, think about it. The karmic implications for Americans in Vietnam can't be good."

"But I was always on the Vietcong's side! I have clippings from my student protest days to prove it!"

"The Vietnamese aren't going to look at your clippings, Leon. To them you're just going to be another middle-aged Ugly American Capitalist Pig. I mean, come on, whether you like it or not, that's who you now are."

I was returning my attention to the trades when I happened to see, out of the corner of my eyes, Leon's expression. In the years I'd known him, I had never seen a look like that. He appeared to be stricken, absolutely stricken, and I immediately regretted what I had said. I should have known better, but it was as if I no longer had that gate inside my brain that stops a person from saying horrible, hurtful things. Whatever that gate is called, mine was gone.

"I'm sorry," I said quickly, forcing the almost forgotten feelings of remorse to come up from inside me. "Oh, Leon. I'm *really* sorry."

"Forget it," he said, and pointedly put his headset on and turned his chair away from me, fixing his gaze on the computer screen. "File it under Another Bad Idea, Louie. Scratch it. Now let me get some work done, for a change."

I rose and moved towards the door and didn't look back even when I thought I might have heard Leon start to cry.

IF I knew my colors better I could tell you what that strip is on the horizon—maybe a royal blue—and how it is subtly different from the rest of the sky and in a very short time, it will grow and expand, making all the stars disappear. Just like Hollywood, right? Stars come and stars go. Maybe Baxter will be a star, but he will have to toughen up first. Before he went to sleep he told me what he and his girlfriend, Jewel, had fought about.

"She doesn't believe in me," he had whispered. "Not like you, Peg. You believe in me, don't you?"

Well, the truth is, of course, I don't believe in anyone. Oh yeah, I lay my money on the line and wait for the wheel to stop, but that's different from believing. But how can I tell them that? So instead I murmured the same words I've murmured into countless young men's ears, a tuneless lullaby promising him riches and fame and power and love. All things nobody can promise anyone because, excepting love, they are not anything anyone really has to give. But for some reason, they all believe me, and soon Baxter's breath became steady and his bones almost softened as he lost himself in what I took to be a confident sleep.

"Today, Baxter will win back his Jewel," I whisper, as if saying it will make it so. I like to think of myself as being kind, even if I am hard of heart.

The first seagulls have started to squawk, reminding me it was about this time roughly seven years ago that I watched Leon dive under a not particularly large wave and never resurface. We had spent the night together at what was then his place, but is now mine, drinking Cristal, doing coke, and listening to Hendrix. I was thirty-four years old at the time, which did not seem young to me then, but sounds young to me now. My breasts were just beginning to fall, and the first fine lines spiked out around my eyes. Leon was forty-one. My age now.

"Past forty, your tolerance for bullshit takes an alarming dip, Louie," he had told me that night.

I was sitting next to him on the couch, listening to *Electric Ladyland*, when he suddenly got very quiet and just stared out at the ocean, and I don't know if it was the Cristal or the coke or the overly familiar music or just the proximity of Leon, the intoxicating warmth of his always-beautiful smell that was reminiscent of sawdust and pearls, but something pulled me firmly into what seemed like a deep, dark blue sleep that was too busy to actually be called rest, and when I came out of whatever it was I was in, maybe an hour later, maybe not even that, my head was plastered against Leon's shirt, and his arm was firmly around my shoulder.

I stayed as quiet as I could, because at that moment I could not think of anywhere I wanted to be but right there, so close to the only man I have ever loved.

"You awake?" he asked so softly a shiver shook up my spine, and when I nodded, he slowly pulled away, and that was when I saw the wet spot on his shirt.

"Oh God. I'm sorry. I drooled all over you . . ." I said, feeling heavy and slow from uncompleted dreams and too much wine and drugs.

Leon shrugged as he stood up and stretched.

"That's not drool," he said in a voice I imagined he used with the new boys when he was alone with them. And that's when I felt the dampness around my eyes and an odd heat on my cheeks, and in a rush of horror and shame I realized I had been crying in my sleep. Crying was one of those things I'd had to give up when I became a big power broker in Hollywood.

"Blood in the water! Blood in the water!" Leon used to yell when I expressed any negative emotions. "Good God, Louie! Pull yourself together! You'll attract the sharks!"

But instead of chiding me that night, he just said in that same sweetly hopeless way, "Give me an ideal, Louie."

"What?" I asked, wiping my eyes.

"An ideal. Any one will do," he said, even softer.

"Okay," I said, but then could not think of a single thing to tell him. I picked up a bottle of Perrier off the floor and took a long drink, hoping to wash the heavy drowsiness out of me; the bubbles felt funny going through my body, more like lightning than liquid.

Leon took off his wet shirt and laid it carefully against the back of the sofa. Then he kneeled down and did something he had never done before, and that was to lightly stroke my cheek with the back of his warm, warm hand. And looking into Leon's beautiful face, so close to mine, I remember it felt like I was in one of those weird movie special effects when the lights suddenly brighten and dim at the same time, putting me at once extremely on edge.

"Guess what, Louie? All this time, we've been playing the wrong parts in the wrong story," Leon said, looking right into my eyes. "Fuck *Casablanca*."

Then Leon kissed me—a chaste, gentle, almost what one could call pretty kiss, before dropping his pants and going out to the beach. Alone.

THE SKY is now pale and the water no longer black but partly a dark, I guess what you might call sea green. It's going to be a cold swim today, but I have no choice. Another split of champagne gone, and I can hear Baxter shifting in the bed. He's a definite type, and if he sticks with the acting lessons and has a few good breaks, he could make it in a Tom Cruise kind of a way, but he could just as easily not. He's sweet, but I don't think I want to sleep with him anymore. I've had my share of sweetness. I need some real nourishment.

The boys I signed right after Leon's death used to ask me about him. I mean, he was a legend in the industry, having launched the careers of many very big stars, but after a while nobody seemed to talk about him anymore because, really, it's pointless to be a legend in Hollywood. You have no value, dead or alive, if you're not somehow making somebody a lot of money.

My thesis on the Chinese Revolution did not go into the dark years that followed the CCP attaining control of the country. I didn't delve into the Cultural Revolution, Gang of Four, One Hundred Flowers. That was a conscious choice because I wanted to come out of college high on hope. Leon, on the other hand, left Berkeley with the radical left already in ruins. He came to Hollywood a cynic, anxious to make a living off the only other thing he was good at besides organizing student demonstrations, which was picking up beautiful boys. Two different starting points, yet here I am, almost in the same spot as Leon when he took the big dive under.

"Beware," I whisper to both no one and everyone. "All roads in Hollywood lead here."

I had no idea how rich Leon was until he died and left everything to me, and I have given a lot, a lot, a lot of that money to political causes I think Leon would want to support, but lately, I find myself thinking of ways I could've saved Leon with all of the money he had, that is now mine. My current favorite is one in which Leon and I buy a big hunk of land in Montana, and become the Ma and Pa of the dude ranch and sleep with all the gorgeous cowboys, who wouldn't ever have to be told how gorgeous they are because that isn't the point with real cowboys, and we'd ride horses and learn to fish, and every day we'd decide on something new and delicious to cook before opening the fridge and finding it filled with a seemingly endless supply of fresh, red meat.

SMALL

TECHNICALLY, THEY WEREN'T REALLY dwarfs, the seven relatively-average-except-for-their-height men whose house in the mountains above Santa Cruz I shared during the summer of 1975, between my freshman and sophomore years in college. What happened was, just before the end of spring quarter, my father, a man of not inconsiderable wealth, who was on his way to visit some South African diamond mines he was a major secret investor in, suddenly disappeared when his prop plane crashed. With my father presumed dead, his wife, my evil bitch of a stepmonster, Marni, newly in charge of the family's finances, made it her first order of business to cut me off.

"Fuck you!" I screamed into the dorm hall phone, over the din of competing Joni Mitchell and Boz Skaggs records, trying not to gag on the intermingling smells of Herbal Essences and hashish. "Show me a copy of the fucking will, you bitch!"

"Will, schmill," Marni gleefully singsonged back, and I could practically hear the Bolla Soave and Boursin cheese digesting in her surgically flattened stomach. "Until the body's found, your father isn't even considered dead yet."

I was used to fighting with Marni. As cliché as it sounds, from the moment she stepped into our house on Sunset Plaza Drive, with her tight French jeans, white gold-digger smile, and obviously fake boobs, I hated her guts and she mine. The only difference between this conversation and about a million others was that in the past my father had always been there to defend me, and I was very aware how hollow my words sounded now that he was no longer around.

"If he's not dead, then what exactly is he?" I said with as much force I could muster in my newly weakened position.

"I'd say, fucked, Page. Just like you," Marni giggled, and then there was the sharp ting of what I knew to be a tastelessly huge and heavy gold loop earring clicking against the receiver. "Now, you just have a bitchin' summer, babe."

Penniless, orphaned, and soon-to-be homeless since the quarter was ending in a few days, I was forced to answer an ad in the university newspaper, *City on a Hill Press*, that offered FREE ROOM AND BOARD FOR PERKY BUT WARMHEARTED COLLEGE COED WITH LONG LEGS AND EXCEPTIONAL PEOPLE SKILLS.

I was not at all certain I was what they were looking for, but as the song goes, when you have nothing, you have nothing to lose. The perky and warmhearted part of the deal was what had me the most worried, but being almost six feet tall and weighing like 120 pounds at the time, I knew, at least, my legs would qualify.

As fate would have it, the guy who picked me up hitchhiking on Highway 9 toward Ben Lomond the day I set out to apply for the living position, or whatever it was, just happened to run a chain of massage parlors in San Jose and offered me a summer job on the spot.

"My girls make $100, $125 a day," he bragged.

"But I don't know anything about massage," I told him.

"You know enough," he said, almost driving off the edge of the two-lane mountain road as he stared at my breasts, shown off to their most perky advantage, I hoped, in the sparkly white tube top that went with the matching burgundy latex hot pants I was wearing that beautiful but cool spring day I first saw the dwarfs' house.

IT WAS about a quarter of a mile off the highway and you had to walk along this narrow but well-marked path through a dense forest of redwoods to reach it. The outside of the house was really nothing to write home about: red clapboard, pointy shingled roof, shuttered windows, the front door heavy and oddly marked with deep holes. When knocked on, it made a kind of hopeless sound that gave you no confidence at all. I looked around for a doorbell, but there wasn't one. So I knocked again, as hard as I could, but still the sound was puny and flat and made me feel bad, so when I tried the door and found it unlocked, I decided to go inside.

I'm not sure what I was expecting, but what I saw was nothing like it. In contrast to its rustic exterior, the living room was a mid-'70s version of a James Bond penthouse—all sleek, modern, leather, chrome, and blond wood furniture on gleaming black marble floors. The oblong glass coffee table, possibly an Eames or a very impressive knockoff, sat on a white polar bear rug. Hanging on the walls were modern prints by the same artists my father and his friends collected: Stella, Lichtenstein, Sam Francis. There was a certain smell in the air, one of a particular moneyed indulgence, that I, being my father's daughter, was no stranger to.

"Hello?" I called from the doorway. "Hello?"

My repeated calls were greeted with silence, and since I was feeling cold and hungry, and even though to maintain my weight I basically tried to eat like nothing ever, I slipped back into the gold platform sandals I had sensibly removed for the hike through the woods and walked directly into the kitchen, which was as unexpected in its appearance as the living room, coming straight out of the set of the *Ozzy and Harriet* show, a perfect slice of early idealized '60s suburbia with wallpaper in a chipper nautical theme and appliances from the previous decade, all American-made.

When I opened the Lady Kenmore refrigerator, I saw the only thing inside was half of a multilayered coconut crème cake, which just happened to be my absolute favorite. It had already been divided into seven even sections, but in my state of extreme hunger, I quickly rationalized that one less could not possibly matter and helped myself to the closest slice and ate it right out of my hands.

It was delicious, like the coconut cake of my dreams, made with plenty of vanilla and butter but not overpowered by too many presweetened coconut flakes. A small piece fell to the floor, which was a kind of crème-colored tile, and, figuring no one would notice, I ground it in with the heel of my platform shoe and continued to eat the cake very quickly and had only a couple bites left when it hit me.

Now, I admit, at nineteen, I was certainly no stranger to drugs, but on the other hand, I wasn't like my freshman roommate, an ex-cheerleader from Palisades High who would actually set her alarm to go off in the middle of the night so she could take some pill or another and effectively keep herself in a permanent state of altered reality. I mean, it was 1975 in Santa Cruz, for God's sake: Taking drugs was like breathing air, no big deal. So I smoked a little grass, dropped a few mushrooms, but basically found drugs to be boring, my own personal vice being bedding down visiting rock musicians, particularly drummers, but that's another story. Anyway, almost immediately it became quite clear that there was something in the coconut cake besides cream of tartar, and although I usually hate those kinds of surprises, I was in such a sad and vulnerable state I decided fuck it, I'll just go with it. I mean, how much worse could it possibly make me feel? So, staring at the morsels of cake I still held in my hand, which had started to change colors from off-white to a sickening flaming pink, I staggered into the living room, kicked off my shoes, and passed out on the unbelievably soft and warm polar bear rug.

OBVIOUSLY, THIS all happened a long time ago when, not surprisingly, in many ways I was a very different person from whom I am today—a middle-aged mother, interested in my children's education and the rising property values of the comfortable neighborhood of Los Angeles we wisely bought into during a real estate slump. Like most, when I look back at things I did when I was younger, I am overwhelmed with conflicting feelings of awe and horror.

As you might've guessed, I never told my husband, Albert, a very well-respected molecular biologist, about the summer I lived with the dwarfs. My motto regarding certain aspects of my past has always been what a person doesn't know won't hurt 'em, and for the most part this has served me well, but the fucked-up thing about fate is it doesn't always deal us the exact hand we're prepared to play when we have to play it, and I gladly would've forgotten that summer forever—I mean, completely erased it from my own personal history—and may have actually gotten away with doing just that, if we hadn't decided to take advantage of the current lower interest rates to refinance our house.

Of course, I recognized Grumpy as soon as we stepped into the bank. He was older, sure. His hair was much shorter, and there was now a distinguished peppering of gray in his beard, but his lips were puckered in his trademark scowl, and I instantly sensed the manic discontent festering behind his neat and officious desk.

I don't know if he saw me, or if he did, if he would have even recognized me. Twenty-three years had passed, for God's sake. My hair, which had been dyed an Edie Sedgwick white when I knew him, was now its natural brown, and since I'd given birth to three children my weight had certainly climbed, and my clothes now were the kind worn by a very moderate (in every sense) middle-aged woman and nothing like the glitter-baby garb I favored the summer I lived with that man.

"Oh shit," I gasped, freezing in the bank's doorway, all at once unable to move.

"What's wrong?" my husband asked, more impatient than concerned. To tell you the truth, he was used to me doing things like stopping dead in the middle of doorways. I have never had a very organized mind and things that I've forgotten tend to come back to me at unexpected moments.

I tried to answer, but no words came out. Instead, I turned and walked back out onto Wilshire Boulevard. Annoyed, my husband had no choice but to follow. "What's going on now, Page?"

"I don't feel well," I said, and gazed up at the skyscrapers that loomed, making me feel trapped.

"*What?*" Every bone in my husband's body tensed with impatience. I couldn't meet his eyes and instead looked down at the tips of my black Italian half boots, which were bought on sale at Nordstrom but were still butt-expensive.

"The bank," I said, feebly.

"The bank?" My husband, who is handsome and solid, was clearly not enjoying this moment of irrational uncertainty.

"It must have new carpeting or something. The fumes were about to make me pass out, Alfred. I can't go back in there. I can't!" I vamped, breathlessly.

"Oh Jesus, Page . . . We've already filled out the application and you know I have that conference coming up in Geneva and . . ."

I looked past Alfred's shoulder and could see Grumpy sitting at his desk near the window. He wasn't looking at me. His head was turned the other way, and as he talked on the phone, he swiveled slightly in his chair in a rhythmic way that reminded me what a good dancer he was, better than the other dwarfs on those nights we cleared the living room, rolled up the bearskin rug, and put on Otis Rush and Al Green records, and, really, he looked like just about any guy working that kind of job—neat suit, neat hair—the only difference being his neat and shiny shoes didn't quite touch the floor and the hand holding the phone was the size of a child's of probably eight or, at the most, nine.

THE FIRST thing I remember is the voices.

"Man, are you guys digging on those legs? I mean, are you digging on them?" This was said in a deep voice full of reverence and lust.

"I'm only gonna ask this one more time: Who left the fucking door unlocked?" This voice was higher and kind of whiney—the voice of someone who always wanted to get his own way, but probably rarely did.

"The cake was perfectly evenly divided. Now either someone's not going to get a second piece or we're going to have to recut it, which will not only make one hell of a mess, but I can no longer vouch for the fairness of each portion." This last statement was punctuated with a loud sneeze.

"This is nice. I like it when I can, you know, just kind of *look*," yet another voice whispered, and when I opened my eyes, I saw a very fair, almost pretty young man with bright blue eyes staring straight at my face with wonder. This, I later learned, was Bashful, and when my gaze met his, he blushed a bright, embarrassed red.

"Doc! Doc!" he started to whisper in an urgent way and quickly moved out of my line of vision. "She's awake!"

I was still in the grips of the drug, or drugs, or whatever it was, and it felt as if an invisible blanket of lead was covering me from head to toe, allowing me to do nothing but lie there and stare straight up. As I tried to remember where the fuck I was, my view of the smooth white ceiling was suddenly obscured by the heads of seven men who were apparently now standing over me, looking down with various degrees of curiosity and interest.

The very dark one with the Neil Young forehead—Happy, I found out later—smiled pleasantly and stared at my legs, but, overall, I didn't think I was making a very good first impression.

"She's not a university student," said the one who I later learned was Grumpy. "Strictly junior college material if you ask me."

"No, no. I looked in her purse, man," the one with a very red nose, Sneezy, said, and then sniffled loudly. "She's got a valid UCSC ID."

"Fake," Grumpy sneered.

"You're such a fucking paranoid, man." Dopey, a hippie with an afro and very glazed eyes, suddenly locked eyes with Grumpy and began to shake his head in a menacing way.

"Yeah, well, if you laid off on the 'ludes, man, you might wake up one day and finally smell the coffee," Grumpy retorted, his irritability quickly turning to a quiet but clearly deep rage.

"What the fuck does that mean, man?" Dopey asked, a dangerous edge entering his drug-heavy voice. "*What the fuck are you trying to say, fuck?*"

And then there was a sudden blur of movement, a strange glint of light, and directly above my abdomen, Dopey was now brandishing an extremely lethal-looking machete inches from Grumpy's neck.

I blinked and in that brief second, a cloud gathered above me, and when I reopened my eyes, I saw that Grumpy was not even looking at the machete, but was instead staring deep into Dopey's red-rimmed eyes.

"It means, *man*," Grumpy said, "I'm fucking sick of you being fucking out of it all the time, *man*. It means, you're not pulling your weight around here, *man*. It means"—Grumpy poked a small but obviously strong finger right between Dopey's stoned eyes—"You're fucking dead meat, you fucking slophouse of a human being."

"What the fuck? Put that shit away!" whined Doc, lifting one of his tiny hands to swat at both the machete and Grumpy's finger like they were nothing but pesky flies. He was probably in his midthirties, with a pointed beard and small wire-rimmed glasses that made him look a little like Trotsky, and the way the others all fell silent, I assumed he was their leader.

"I'm fucking sick of all of your bitching all the time," Doc scolded, and looked sternly at Dopey and Grumpy, and then at the other four dwarfs as well. "Now, in case you've forgotten, we have a situation here and I suggest we deal with it. *Someone*, I don't know who, left the fucking door unlocked and, like I said, anyone could've come in here. Do I have to spell this out? *Anyone* could have come in here and been just lying in wait!"

"But *anyone* didn't come in, Doc," Sleepy, the one with soft, light brown curls and tired eyes, said, and then yawned. "Just her."

Everyone turned their attention back to me and I tried to smile.

"Hi," was all I could manage to say, I admit, rather lamely.

At this point, with a small sigh, Doc leaned slightly lower and looked directly in my eyes.

"Okay, this is the deal," he said in a let's-get-down-to-business way. "We need a woman to live here to kind of neutralize the male energy of the house before we all kill each other. You don't have to do anything. No cooking, cleaning, sexual favors, or mending torn garments. We have a secret gold mine that we toil in most of the day, so that time is yours to do what you choose, but you can't entertain friends here or ever give out this phone number. There's a nice lady who lives down the hill who will take important messages for you, but just don't drink any tea she offers. You have your own room with your own TV, stereo, and electric typewriter, and you can like us or hate us, but just never show any favoritism, because jealousy, real or imagined, will only add to what I can only describe as the very volatile nature of the relationship we have with each other. So, what do you say?"

THE OTHER girls who worked the day shift at Touch 'n' Go, the massage parlor in San Jose, were pretty much what you would expect. Gina was a graduate student in East Asian studies at Stanford. Marcy was doing her postdoctorate work in economics at Cal, and Candy, the junkie, told us she had once been a child-prodigy classical violinist before the insane pressure sent her running into the warm, comforting arms of hard narcotics abuse at the tender age of twelve. I liked them all well enough but never saw them out of the workplace, taking my obligations seriously at the dwarfs' house and always hitchhiking straight home so I could be there for the guys when they came back from what I later learned was really a secret marijuana field somewhere in the Santa Cruz Mountains.

It turned out that Dick, the owner of the massage parlor, had greatly exaggerated the earning power of the job. Candy, who had her habit to consider and would thusly do just about anything with anyone, was the exception, but me and Gina and Marcy rarely brought home more than $50 a day and in my case it was usually closer to $25 or $30. It wasn't like we were snobs or prudes. We knew what was expected (basically everything but penetration) and tried to do our job with a good attitude and always removed our glasses and lowered our diction so the customers wouldn't be made to feel intellectually inferior in any way, but for some reason we just didn't attract the big spenders.

"Do you think $10 is an adequate tip for a hand job?" Gina and I queried Marcy, assuming her background in economics could help us put this whole thing in perspective as we sat around on the burgundy velour couches in what was called the Hospitality Lounge.

"Depends," Marcy answered, not even looking up from her Hegel, the book she always retreated to between clients, cleverly hidden behind a *Valley of the Dolls* dust jacket.

"Depends on what?" Gina asked, impatiently tapping her pencil on her advanced Mandarin worksheet, carefully camouflaged as a sex-drive questionnaire from a recent issue of *Cosmo*.

"Page?" Marcy looked at me in a condescending way, like a teacher's aide. "Would you like to try to answer Gina's question?"

"Supply and demand," I said, returning to my pile of old *Interview* magazines (which really were just *Interview* magazines), picking up one of my favorites that had the interview Andy Warhol and Bob Colacello did with Keith Moon at Quo Vadis a few years earlier.

Marcy nodded and through the thin wall we could hear Candy's customer, a wiry air-conditioner repairman, cry out in ecstasy. None of us acknowledged it. We each just turned a page and waited for our supply to be in somebody's demand.

MEANWHILE, IN the heart of deepest Africa, my father, who, as I suspect you've already guessed, was not killed in the plane crash, but had merely displaced his shoulder, which healed slowly on its own with time, was rescued from the remote desert site by a band of Kalahari Bushmen who themselves had met with misfortune when they took a wrong turn somewhere on the Zimbabwe border and traveled hundreds of miles northward in their quest for an apparently mythical shortcut back to Botswana.

Returning to a more elemental way of life of hunting, gathering, and seeking protection from predators and bad weather, my father later told me, he was never calmer and happier than the weeks he spent with the Bushmen, whom he described as being very lovely people with the one annoying flaw of having what he called "a very European-style sense of humor," meaning a lot of their jokes' punch lines were simply weird explosion sounds they made with their mouths.

The only thing that marred his otherwise tranquil existence was a recurring nightmare in which it was I, not he, who had somehow become lost in a strange foreign land where every

night wild beasts nibbled on small pieces of my heart, never
enough to kill me, just slowly and surely, little by little, taking
away the essence of what had once been the person he had
known as me.

So was I happy in the time I lived with the dwarfs? Well, let's
put it this way: I wasn't too unhappy. I missed my father, of
course. And I missed being in L.A. in the summer, lying by
the pool, the heat, the dirty air, picking up musicians at the
Whiskey and Rainbow, the beach, and, as we later learned, its
carcinogenic surf. I did not, of course, miss Marni, who—I
heard from my dad's old secretary, Rita, when I called to give
her the phone number of the lady who lived down the hill—
was now dating my orthodontist, a totally sleazy character
whose offices were in Panorama City, for God's sake.

And what about the dwarfs? How did they feel about me?
Well, as far as I could tell, once I was ensconced in their
house, their feelings ran the complete spectrum from contempt (Grumpy) and indifference (Sleepy) to out-and-out
lust (Happy) and painful infatuation (Bashful). I soon discovered that Doc and Sneezy were actually a pretty solid couple,
and Dopey was a confirmed bisexual cross-dresser, his prefer-
ence in both partners and undergarments dictated by whatever drug he happened to be on at the moment.

I liked them. All of them, even Grumpy. They were weird,
that's for sure. I suspect a lot of that weirdness came from their
shared lack of height, but as a group, they were extremely
well-read (particularly in nineteenth-century Russian litera-
ture), had pretty good taste in music (one of the few things
they could all agree upon was that disco sucked), and, when

they weren't on some kind of paranoid, homicidal rage, they were really a lot of fun to hang with.

One night when Doc and I were the last up, sharing a small bottle of Courvoisier while we listened to *Rastaman Vibration*, he explained it all to me.

"We met when we were all recruited to join the clown army of a famous circus troupe that every spring sends scouts out to scour the country in search of people of small stature, offering promises of not only wealth and fame, but guaranteed student loans to institutions of higher learning of our choice." Doc paused to bring the snifter to his nose and savor the essence of the cognac in a rather long and, I thought, pretentious way.

"But once signed up and living in what the circus called their 'boot camp,' which was actually just a depressing old Motel 6 in southern Florida with an adjacent empty lot where they'd put three rusting circus rings, we immediately sensed the older and truly small clowns, the bona fide dwarfs and midgets, harbored a deep resentment against us new recruits," Doc continued. "They thought—no doubt rightly so—that we were trying to cash in on what was their legitimate turf and conspired to torture us with an endless barrage of cruel practical jokes until finally, one night, having had enough, we piled into Sneezy's '55 pickup and headed west where Dopey hoped, with our help, he would be able to realize his dream of becoming a major drug kingpin by his thirtieth birthday."

Doc paused to take a hit of the joint he was smoking alone, and I slowly ran my hand along the fine stubble just beginning to grow out on my legs stretched out before me on the bear rug, and wondered if my earning power at the massage parlor would improve if I splurged on a leg waxing.

"As growers, our success almost immediately exceeded our greatest expectations," Doc continued, now in a grass-raspy voice, reclaiming my attention from the hair on my legs. "But, sadly, this kind of success does not come without a price, and as you probably already suspected, there are many people now who would rather see us dead than to continue to feel belittled by our unbelievable good fortune. So, it is basically a matter of survival that we all continue to stick together— there being, of course, the safety in numbers factor to consider, but also none of us trust the others enough to allow anyone to leave the group, for fear they will divulge the exact whereabouts of our marijuana field and possibly give away our secret and simple but highly effective gardening tips."

Doc gave me one of those sage looks that I strongly suspected he practiced in the mirror, and I nodded drunkenly before asking, "Did anyone ever tell you, Doc, you look an awful lot like Trotsky?"

THEN ONE day, when Alfred was away at a convention in Geneva and the kids were in school, I called the bank. It was like something I could not help doing, and it wasn't until the switchboard operator picked up that I realized I didn't know Grumpy's real name. That was one of the rules of the house: I was only to know them by their "code names."

"Oh, hi," I fumbled. "Um . . . I want to speak to someone who works at your bank. I can't remember his name but he's really short. I mean, like *really* short."

"One second please," the switchboard operator said, and before I knew it, the phone was ringing and then I heard Grumpy's unmistakable cold, tense voice.

"Auto and Recreational Vehicle Loans. How may I help you?"

"Grumpy?" I said softly, and then I didn't say anything more.

He didn't say anything either, and I could almost hear the annoyed expression souring his face before he muttered, "Well! Well! Well! I was wondering when you would finally call."

EXCEPT FOR the girls I worked with, my life that summer was almost exclusively populated by men, and at night, after I undressed slowly with the lights on and the shades up, inhaling the cool, clean, pine-scented air, doing a kind of striptease while pretending not to notice the red-tipped joint being passed around in the yard, I'd lie down and close my eyes and invariably feel a sudden and intense wave of maleness wash over me, my ears filling with their deep voices, fingers grasping their hard muscles, nostrils flaring against their earthy scent, mouth awash with their mild and salty taste. It was not unpleasant, this sensation, and for that brief moment there was almost a kind of transference of a no-questions-asked strength into me, but after the wave subsided I would be left feeling completely empty and alone and sometimes I cried because I missed my father as badly as I ever had as a child, wanting terribly to feel safe and taken care of again, because really, for the first (and now I can say only) time in my life, that one summer, I was completely on my own, and so it was that, with a hopeless desire to negate that very truth, I would find myself, almost against my will, climbing out of bed and tiptoeing across the now quiet house to one darkened room or another, where whomever it was would be waiting for me, so sweet and warm and small under the covers, short but strong arms partly open, as if with the sole purpose of pulling me close.

It was at the Starbucks across the street from his bank that Grumpy and I agreed to meet. I got there a little early and was waiting outside when I saw him crossing Wilshire among a large crowd of pedestrians and was struck once again by how small he really was. He looked like a child weirdly dressed up as a businessman for Halloween, and I kept waiting for the woman (obviously a complete stranger) in the neat black pants suit walking beside him to reach out and protectively take his hand.

When Grumpy stepped up on the curb, I smiled and waited for some kind of physical contact usually exchanged by people who have not seen each other for a long time— a hug or handshake even—but Grumpy just moved quickly past, opening the coffeehouse's door so that the thick scent of freshly roasted coffee could press full force against me and said, "Whatever you do, don't order a *short*-size drink."

There was one free table in the back of the crowded Starbucks and so we headed there with our tall nonfat latte (mine) and grande cap with extra foam (his). Once we were settled, Grumpy turned his chair so he wouldn't have to look directly at me and said, "Don't ask me what happened."

I just looked at him and stirred a brown packet of natural sugar into my coffee and wondered if he had gotten more cranky with age or if I had just forgotten how totally unpleasant he could be.

"I'll just tell you this much," he continued, taking a sip of his drink, the large paper cup looking dangerously heavy in his tiny hands. "It was an inside job. That's all I'll tell you."

I REALLY did try hard to adhere to Doc's directive not to show any favoritism, and with this in mind, I admit to sleeping with all the dwarfs—although in the case of Doc and Sneezy, that's all we did, sleep, the three of us comfortably cuddled together in Sneezy's Kleenex-littered bed. And I have to tell you, seven was such a perfect number for sleeping around— there being, of course, a night in the week for each dwarf— that I quite honestly believe I had no favorites. I mean, I could kind of get into whatever it was that the dwarf of the night was into, which for the most part was pretty much what most guys are into, to lesser or greater degrees, but all too soon I became aware of a whiff of unfounded jealousy hanging in the air, starting with a constant low-level bickering over things like wet towels left on bathroom floors, but soon worsening until all conversation during dinner stopped. Everyone just began to stare at his plate and eat. At first, I tried to bring up engaging topics, such as a certain amusing quirk of one of my customers that day, or to launch what I hoped would be a lively debate on the relative merits of Gorky's versus Chek-hov's short stories, but my attempts were met with grunts and shrugs.

After dinner, instead of congregating in the living room for brandy and cigars as was their habit, the dwarfs began to go to their rooms, where they listened to records, usually Jimi Hendrix or Cream, worked on their memoirs, or raided the medicine cabinet for downers, taking them by the handful and passing out wherever they fell.

And so it was, what with the increased tension in the household and the growing uncertainty weighing on my shoulders, knowing that the fall quarter would soon be upon me and that I hadn't saved anywhere near enough money to cover my tuition, that by the end of the summer my skin started to break out alarmingly, which may have accounted for my lack of attention when the lady who picked me up hitchhiking to work one morning said, "You're in love."

"What?" I said, partly because it was hard to hear over the loud whine of the old rust-colored Beetle's engine and partly because it was still morning and morning, either early or late, has never been my best time and partly because I was trying to pop a hideous but stubborn pimple I had just noticed on my chin.

"You're in love. I can tell," the wild-haired lady repeated, without even looking at me.

"No, I'm not in love," I said, sleepily wiping the tiny drop of pus into the palms of my hands. "I'm just having a lot of sex this summer."

"It suits you," the freaky lady said, still not taking her eyes off the road, riding the bumps with a kind of grace I had to admire.

"Yeah, well, to tell you the truth, I'd rather have less sex and a greater sense of security in my life."

"Granted."

"What?"

"You got your wish," she said simply, and suddenly in my

mind all of the sex with the multitude of partners (customers and dwarfs) was taken away from me like a platter of food
before I could do more than taste it and I was about to say
something like, well, maybe not, I mean, a little more of a lot
of sex wouldn't be too bad, but the lady had already stopped
the car at the Highway 17 on-ramp, the one that headed north
toward San Jose, and was reaching into a bag of groceries she
had in the backseat, handing me a bright red apple.

Holding the apple, I slowly climbed out of the Beetle, and
as soon as I shut the car's squeaky door, the lady shouted something I couldn't quite understand, maybe, "Bon appetite," or it
could have been, "Watch your feet," before she drove away as
quickly as one could in a beat-to-shit Bug.

Well, I hadn't had any breakfast or much of a dinner the
night before, Sneezy having (hostilely, I suspected) fixed a big
casserole of stuffed peppers, a dish that no one but he and
Doc liked, so I couldn't stop myself from immediately taking
an enormous bite out of the apple and was, of course, startled
when a piece of paper fell straight from its core.

Squinting, I kneeled down and saw even before picking it
up that scrawled under the heading A SPECIAL MESSAGE FOR
YOU were the words, *I'm back* —Dad.

Realizing that the woman who had just picked me up must
have been our message-taking neighbor only after I had swallowed the bite of apple, I braced myself for I didn't know
what (it turned out to be a very mild stomachache) and stared
at the message I now held in my hand as I simply crossed the
road and started to hitchhike in the opposite direction, south,
not north, hoping to go back to the way I used to be, another

spoiled L.A. rich girl who had been indulged in all the wrong ways, thus giving me a roughly fifty-fifty chance of ever amounting to anything in this world before nightfall.

So THAT is how it ended, that summer. Without so much as a good-bye, I exited the dwarfs' lives and they mine and for a short time I alleviated my guilt by figuring that since what they had to offer, the free room and board, was such a good deal, they'd easily find a replacement for me. Plus, I thought, with some minor alterations, Dopey would really enjoy the clothes I had left behind.

Once back in L.A. (where I managed to blend what remained of the witchy lady's apple into Marni's breakfast smoothie one morning, giving her a terrible case of gas that lasted for days), I was pleased to learn that my father, his consciousness newly raised by his experiences in Africa, had divested all of his politically questionable holdings and even went so far as to donate his not-unimpressive modern art collection to the Black Panther Party.

The months I had spent with the dwarfs quickly came to seem like a dream—the kind that is with you so strongly in the morning it has almost physical proportions but by noon is all but forgotten—as I made up for lost time, working hard on my tan, shopping at Fred Segal, and hanging out every night at the Roxy and Starwood, and so you can imagine my surprise when one morning, just a few days before the start of fall quarter, I woke up late and opened the *L.A. Times* only to see a picture of what looked like the smoldering remains of the dwarfs' house on around page seven in the News of the

State section, with the headline FIVE KILLED IN REMOTE
SANTA CRUZ HOUSE. Then, in smaller print, it said DRUG
WAR SUSPECTED.

IT TOOK us a ridiculously long time to finish our drinks,
Grumpy and me, the time going by slowly due to our utter
lack of conversation. Finally, when there were just the gritty
remains of finely ground coffee at the bottom of our cups, I,
trying hard not to sound too forced and rehearsed, said, "Well
Grumpy, isn't it funny to think of who we were and what
we've become?"

I smiled pleasantly, but Grumpy just shot me an annoyed
look and said, "No."

I paused as Grumpy continued to glare, as if daring me to
say anything else that might further annoy him, and really, I
would've liked to just walk out right then, maybe go straight
to my children's school and stand outside the fence until I
caught a glimpse of them, safe, happy, and at play with their
friends, but I forced myself to stay where I was and continued,
now in an even softer voice.

"I guess my point is, I would never cast blame on anyone
for doing what they felt they had to do when they had to do
it," I said.

"It wasn't me," Grumpy said suddenly.

"What?" I asked, startled.

"Some bad speed and a pair of too-tight panties sent that
poor, stupid fuck Dopey right over the edge one night." And
for the first time, Grumpy actually looked sad, but a lot of
time had passed, and as we all know, time dulls the sharpness

of our brightest memories as well as the most biting pain, intensity having no longevity whatsoever, and in what seemed like a flash, Grumpy's expression returned to normal.

"Oh . . . well . . ." I said, wondering two things: (1) If Grumpy was as innocent as he claimed, how did he manage to escape the same fate as the other poor, doomed dwarfs? And, (2) had Dopey been wearing a pair of my left-behind panties when he went over the edge? But even as these questions rushed through my head, I knew with complete certainty that I was better off never knowing for sure.

"Oh . . . well," I repeated, and took a deep breath and forced myself to speak in a neutral but still friendly way. "It has been delightful to see you again, Grumpy, but I'm afraid I must ask a small favor before I go."

Grumpy said nothing, but just looked at me, his expression also neutral, but not at all friendly.

"I would like you never to tell anyone who I once was to you, and you to me, that together we agree to completely forget that we ever knew each other and from this moment forward, be nothing more than strangers, okay?"

For a second, Grumpy looked disappointed with my request. And I wondered what he had been hoping I would ask, but before I could say another thing, Grumpy had jumped off of his chair and was straightening the collar of his suit and looking at a woman who was tall and thin and dressed only in a leotard that made her look catlike as she impatiently searched for something inside her large leather bag and said, "Deal."

ONE VERY hot day in the beginning of August of the said summer, Candy the junkie and I were alone together in the

Hospitality Lounge of the Touch 'n' Go, Marcy having recently quit when she was offered a job as CFO of a small start-up computer company, and Gina having decided to take the day off to entertain some visiting Chinese scholars with a tour of San Francisco's Fisherman's Wharf and a leisurely stroll across the Golden Gate Bridge.

"So, what's it like doing it with a dwarf?" Candy asked, and glanced impatiently at the front door, trying to will the arrival of another perverted customer who would ask her to perform strange and sickening acts for which he would pay through the nose.

"They aren't really dwarfs," I said, trying not to sound too defensive. "They're just small. That's all."

"How small?" Candy asked, and sleepily scratched her arm the way all junkies tend to do.

"About five feet," I guessed.

"That's really weird," she said, now scratching the other arm. "What?"

"A bunch of small guys all living together. Something's really weird about that."

"Actually, in most respects, they're really normal. I mean, if you were around them for a while you'd just forget how small they are. That's just how it happens."

"Is it?" she said, and looked at me in such a way that for the first time I could see her as she might have once been, sans the black circles under her eyes, unhealthy pallor, and permanently chapped lips, a child prodigy out-sized by what must have been a painfully enormous talent.

"So, what's it like?" she asked again, almost too focused for comfort, and I shrugged and wondered, *why is she acting like*

I'm the weirdo? I mean, she's the junkie who'll pee in a complete stranger's mouth for the right price.

I got up and walked across the forest green shag carpet, opened the refrigerator, and helped myself to a bright pink can of Tab. I popped open the top, took a long drink, and gazed out the window at the bar across the street, the one with the broken front door and rain-spotted windows and thought, even as I stared, *I will never remember the name of that place*, before I finally answered, "Nice."

THE OLD BEAN

ECAUSE I AM AT least twenty years older than most of my co-workers, I have made it clear that if there is only one seat available during our breaks, it belongs to me.

"This is not a question of comfort," I tell them. "This is about survival!"

Not that I think any of my co-workers could give a fuck if I survive this job at the Old Bean or not.

You are such a fucking loser, I can read in their eyes as they gaze at me during down moments without interest. And what can I say, except they are probably right. I don't think there are a lot of super-together, high-powered women in their midforties making cappuccinos for college students five hours a day, five days a week, but who knows? Maybe there are. Maybe there are legions of us, returning to an indifferent job market with our rusty people skills and long-ago-earned degrees. Maybe everywhere there are women like me who, after years inside the home, raising our kids, tending to the needs of our families, feeling the colors that once made us vibrant slowly pale like that cheap color film we all used and so now have boxes of only sucky photos of ourselves when we actually looked pretty good, wake up one morning with a need for maybe a little validation, just a little, and are willing to accept that validation in the form of measly paychecks and the few dollars that come out of the tip jar after it is split four ways. Maybe there are millions of us, secretly happy to be asked to perform simple repetitive tasks and to do them well, tasks that carry very little consequential weight, unlike those nebulous ones that were essential to raising what we hoped would become somewhat sane people and keeping our husbands in love with us. Maybe there are *billions* of us, hogging the sole empty stool at the end of the counter, sipping a cup of decaf sweetened with Equal and watching the hands of the clock, wishing the fifteen-minute break could somehow expand like our waists, thighs, asses almost inevitably did after we crossed over the bridge to forty. But somehow I doubt it.

I AM not the only old gal working at the Old Bean. June Atkinson works three mornings a week and she is even older than I am. I would guess she was in her midsixties, but she could be in her seventies, or even eighties. June is an older woman in the same vein as Big Martha, Martha Stewart's tiny, irascible mother who is ninety but has more energy and spunk than most of my younger co-workers. June is small and smiley, but her hearing is not good, and so when she works the cash register, she often gets the orders mixed up and causes a lot of extra work for the rest of us—the remaking of regular lattes into nonfat ones, the dumping out of soy-cocoas and replacing them with whip cream–less mochas, that sort of thing, but the customers clearly like her. She is, by far, the most friendly, and so Laurel, our manager, often puts her in the position where she can interact with the public—the place, to my building resentment, where Laurel puts me the least.

"Why do you think she's doing this?" I ask my husband during one of our almost-daily phone calls that are supposed to bridge the geographical gap between where he now lives, "on the other side of the pond," and where I continue to live, here, because moving with him would have meant many things that I could not deal with at the time. He, unlike me, is a person who never lost his focus, and even though the road has not always been completely smooth, he does have a real job, a career even, one filled with exciting challenges, rewarding problems to solve, real responsibilities, and a quite-respectable salary. I know he doesn't take my job seriously, and really, why should he? But still, it kind of hurts my feelings when he answers my question with a completely indifferent "Gee, Penny . . . maybe she hates your guts."

AND MAYBE she does.

Although she shouldn't.

When there are lulls in the crowds, I always find constructive things to do like clean the blades in the coffee grinders, or restock the bins with dark, grease-shiny beans that come out of heavy, slippery/scratchy burlap bags that smell faintly of hay and wreak havoc with one's nails. I even volunteer to do the most dreaded task of all, going out into the horrible, creepy, smelly alley to throw away the used grounds. I do all these things partly because I know they have to get done, but also because, unlike my other co-workers (Manager Laurel included) who, when there are no immediate orders to fill, huddle together and bond over things like recent bad dates and graduate school applications, I have no one to bond with.

Of course, the natural candidate for friendship would be the other old person, June Atkinson, but in her own sweet way, June has made it clear that she isn't really interested in being my friend. She always answers my questions with short, polite responses but never really meets my eye or poses any questions of her own, and at the first possible moment she hurries off to the backroom where she throws herself into her seemingly never-ending project known as inventory. And I, pulling out the box of strawberry scones and restocking the pastry case, realize that except for both being old, we, meaning me and June, may not really have anything else in common and, well, how compelling is age as a reason for friendship anyway?

I TALK to my husband almost every day, but I have to force myself to refrain from calling my daughter, Teddy, more than once a week. Even though my husband, Phillip, and I have never acknowledged it, we both know the biggest reason I did not move with him overseas was Teddy. To admit to that would be to admit to still having the concerns that we try to tell ourselves have been put to rest. The medication has worked miracles. Teddy's new roommate appears to be sweet and responsible. In her guarded way, Teddy's therapist has reassured me that Teddy's condition is improving. Her grades are good again and the boy, the one that started this whole, well, *mess*, transferred to another college out of state. Everything seems to be okay, but how can I trust what I cannot see? How can all that I do not and cannot know reassure me?

"Tell me everything is going to be all right," I demand of the dog, who lies beside me on the bed, she and I the last two occupants of what was once, not very long ago really, what I thought to be a pretty happy family home.

"Tell me everything is going to be fine," I say to the black-and-white mutt, who opens her mouth only to yawn.

I COME into the Old Bean one morning and find a new kid behind the espresso machine. He is, someone explains when we are in the backroom tying on long green aprons and punching our time cards, a night guy who's been called in to substitute for Kay because she sprained her wrist skateboarding the day before.

"God, I hate when I do that," I say just as Laurel comes into the backroom and directs me to join the new guy making drinks.

"But," I protest, because I've actually started to keep track of the rotations and technically it is my turn to work the cash register. It's my turn to smile and say hello to the customers. It's my turn for a possibility of a little "lite" but friendly interaction with people other than the mostly glum, self-involved kids who are my co-workers. It's my turn not to burn my hands and breathe in endlessly thick espresso fumes. It's my turn to play with the computerized ordering system and call out names and hand out drinks and actually be thanked. It's my turn!

"No butts here, sweetie, only assholes like me," Laurel says in a chipper way, doing the equivalent of calling something "my bad," taking the blame, but still leaving *me* feeling totally ripped off.

Glumly, I take my place beside the new guy who immediately stops steaming the small, metal pitcher of milk he seems to have been steaming for too long anyway. He holds out his hand and introduces himself as Special Ed.

"Hi," I mumble, still stunned by Laurel's easy and efficient handling of me as I distractedly shake this kid's hand that is warm and soft and slightly damp from I assume the over-steaming. The air that hovers around the espresso machine is humid and smells of espresso beans, burnt and razor-sharp. I glance longingly at the cash register and for the first time notice the pretty big crowd waiting for their drinks. Then I look at the computer screen beside the coffee machine and am taken aback by the number of orders to be filled.

"You haven't done these yet?" I ask the kid, hoping to hear an explanation about the malfunctioning computer, watch a finger point to the bottom of the list at the place we're really at, reassurance that things aren't as fucked up as I think they are.

"Yeah," the kid says. "I mean, no. I mean, we still have to make those drinks. I mean, see that? Those are the drinks we've got to make. Man, people really drink a lot more coffee in the morning than they do at night, don't they? Who are you, anyways?"

I look at the kid and see that he is a kind of lost boy from another era: dyed-black, spiked-up hair, pale white skin, studded belt, but with no visible tattoos or piercings. His eyes are bright and there is a kind of sweet eagerness in his expression that I have not seen on any of the other kids' faces before. When he smiles, he reveals an ordeal of a mouth, and I can't help but wonder where his parents were during the years of orthodontics.

This kid is a disaster, I realize, and of course, Manager Laurel has assigned me to work with this disaster, because, as my husband has already rightly pointed out, she obviously hates me. And why does this girl hate me? What have I done to engender such antipathy? Nothing, as far as I can see. Laurel hates me because she fears becoming what I am, which in her eyes is probably aimless and old. Oh, Jesus! Who needs this? Certainly not me! I turn my back to the fucked-up kid and endless list of unfilled orders and spot Laurel, oblivious to the mess that we are in, talking in the corner with this other little girl, Pietra, who is also really snitty to me and whose hair I've never seen because she always, *always* wears the same disgusting dirty handkerchief tied pirate-style over her head, but before I can storm over and throw my stupid apron right in their smug, perpetually self-satisfied faces, the new kid reaches out and stops me.

"Hey," he says, strangely insistently. "I said, who are you?"

I am about to tell him that he doesn't need to know who I am because I am quitting and we will never see each other again and that long list of orders that he has somehow let go unfilled is, unfortunately, his problem, when I happen to look at him again, him with his antiquated hairdo and pale skin and miserable mouth, but those eyes. Those (are they blue or gray?) eyes that unlike the eyes of the other kids who work here, which seem to have gone prematurely dead with extreme cynicism, are alive, really alive, and are, at that moment, regarding me in a way no one has regarded me in so long that I almost forget what it means to be looked at that way. Almost.

"I'm the best thing that never happened," I hear myself quote one of my all-time favorite songs, and immediately feel it, my determination to quit slipping out of me, falling to the floor, puddling around my feet.

"Hey! Westerberg, right? Was that song on the second or third solo album?" Special Ed surprises me by correctly identifying the songwriter of the really pretty obscure song. "Man, I love Paul Westerberg! He's like my idol, man. Or one of my idols. I have like fifty of 'em. Is that too many? Do you think I should kind of cull my idol list? It might kind of cheapen the whole idol status if there's like too many like all crammed into the same hotel bed, right? But the Replacements, man! They are like my all-time fucking favorite idols . . ."

"Yes. I love them too," I say, because it's true, and as I have done many times before, feel myself falling a little bit in love with the person who loves one of the same things that I do.

"Wow. This is just too cool," the kid says, and despite the list of drinks, he just continues to stand there, his long arms hanging uselessly beside his torso, looking at me with even more of what he was looking at me with before.

Who he reminds of is the kind of boy I would have fallen in love with back in the late 1970s. The kind who would have so thoroughly and efficiently broken my heart and left me in almost as bad of a shape as my daughter was in last year after that horrible boy, that Lewis, that creep, that demon, smoked her precious, innocent heart to smithereens. But, I also realize, I am not young. I am not vulnerable. This boy cannot hurt me and so, if he can't hurt me, what in the world does he want with me, anyway?

"In case you haven't noticed, I'm old enough to be your mother," I feel compelled to point out.

"Yeah. I noticed. So?"

"So . . . you shouldn't flirt with me. If that *is* what you are doing?"

"Am I flirting with you?" He appears to consider the question seriously. "Well, yeah . . . I probably am. I mean, that is kind of what I do . . ."

"Flirt?"

"Yeah. See. I can't really control it. I just need everyone to love me too much. That's kind of my character flaw. It's no big deal, really . . . So, like, what do you want to do?" he asks with that charming eagerness, as if we were on a date and I am to choose between going to a movie or out to hear some music, and he is basically up for anything as long as it is with me.

This kid, I decide, must be insane. But who am I? This middle-aged woman who has raised an emotionally shaky child, whose husband now lives over ten thousand miles away, whose friends have distanced themselves since the ugliness of the previous year, or maybe it was me who distanced myself from them, but in any case could not be described as being caught up in a whirlwind of a social life. Who am I to cast judgment?

"How 'bout we maybe fill those orders," I say, and his mouth explodes as if I had suggested the best, most fun, most exciting thing he has ever heard.

"Cool!" he says.

Although it has not been an entire week since my last call (one that she still has not returned), I call my daughter Teddy when I get home from work. She does not answer, but her roommate, Liz, does and tells me that Teddy is at her Spanish class, and I am not entirely sure I believe her.

"So . . . how are things?" I ask Liz, instead of what I really want to ask, which is "How is Teddy?" because I'm trying to be, well, cool.

"Things are really good. I really like my classes this quarter and I'm writing film reviews for the school paper, which means I can see all of the terrible movies before anyone else and then I get to tell everyone how terrible they are first and I've been on the South Beach and lost four pounds but I'm having awful cravings for pretzels dipped in peanut butter and jelly . . ."

"And Teddy?" I interrupt, unable to appear cool another second. "How is she?"

"Oh . . . yeah, Teddy? She seems . . . great," Liz reports in what sounds like an insincere way, but I realize this girl always sounds a little insincere. That is probably what makes her seem so nice.

I want to demand an elaboration. I want hard evidence of Teddy's "greatness." I want details, names, places, descriptions of defining events and moments, but I say instead, "Well, tell her to call me, okay?"

"Will do," Liz says, still with no real sincerity, which I take to be a good sign but realize that it probably isn't.

"A KID flirted with me yesterday," I tell my husband when he calls the next morning, which is the next night for him. He, as usual, sounds tired and quite possibly drunk and very definitely like he would prefer not to be talking to me.

"What kid?" he asks without interest, and tries to hide the fact that he has turned on the TV by immediately muting the sound, but not fast enough. I heard it, the flash of music, the sharp hum of the foreign airwaves.

"This kid at work. His name is Special Ed. He looks kind of like you a long time ago, but worse . . ."

"When are you coming here, Penny?" Phil interrupts, speaking in a weary way, as always not the least bit interested in what happened to me at my work. Even a flirting boy doesn't pique his interest, which both annoys me and makes me feel relieved.

"I'm not sure," I answer honestly.

"I spoke to Ted today. She sounded good."

"You called her?"

"Nah . . . she called me. Sounded real happy. Said she was going to a beach party this weekend. Says she might want to go to law school. Says . . . well, she sounds fine, Penny."

"Law school?" I say, and have to keep myself from sounding as jealous as I feel. Teddy never calls me. I always have to call her and when we do speak she basically tells me nothing. *Nothing.* But she seems to call her father often and appears to have real, substantial conversations with him. Her father, who, I feel compelled to point out, did not sacrifice himself, his life, his career for her, yet is still the one she obviously longs for. "Teddy is thinking about *law* school?"

"That's what she said . . . Boy oh boy, you are really going to like it here, Pen." Phil is smart enough to know to switch the subject off of Teddy. "The food. The wine. The food. The wine. The food. The wine."

"You know, I do care about things other than food and wine, Phil," I say, still feeling all cruddy.

"Like what?" he challenges.

"Teddy," I sigh in resignation. *Oh Teddy, come and sit on my lap and be my girl again. Oh, Teddy . . .*

"Teddy is doing fine," Phil tells me again, all at once sounding even more tired than before. "She's a kid who went through a hard time, but that happens. Put it in perspective, Penny. The past is the past. It's over and now she is doing fine. Name another."

"Well . . . I care about you."

"So, guess what? *I'm* here. Food, wine, and *me*. What more could anyone want? Food, wine and *me* . . ."

Because I do not know what anyone could want more than that, I say nothing.

THE NEXT time I see Special Ed, I brace myself. I must act as I think I should, less available, more mature, barely approachable. But when I walk into work, he doesn't even say hello and I am left standing there, stunned and shaken by the snub, watching as he walks up to this exceptionally pretty girl, Madeline, and eagerly begins to show her these black-and-white photos of musicians in the '70s and '80s that I overhear him say he just bought for a few bucks at a flea market.

Madeline, a small, dark woman who has the bone structure of a rare bird and a kind of detached quality that, when I think about it, I realize a lot of my co-workers also share, which then forces me to wonder if they might all be on the same kind of medication as Teddy, the one that mutes all of their responses so it's kind of like breaking through sheer layers of ice each time you have a conversation with them, looks at the pictures in the same way one looks at the health department report on a restaurant's wall, without really seeing.

"Okay . . . now, see here, that's Johnny Thunders when he was in the New York Dolls," I overhear Special Ed say excitedly as I put on my apron. I am trying not to pay attention to them because as much as I hate to admit it, it's making me feel weird the way Special Ed is ignoring me, but on my way to refill the sugar dispensers, I just happen to glance at the picture of Johnny Thunders, a kind of unsavory but still vaguely compelling character in a moment of popular culture history that used to, at one time, mean a lot to me, and blurt out, "That's not Johnny Thunders, that's Sylvain Sylvain."

Both Special Ed and Madeline turn and look at me as if I were nothing but someone's old cell phone that was accidentally left on the counter and has started to ring, basically just a rude annoyance, before, together and without a word, they turn back to the pictures, and I (who have gotten used to being ignored by these kids) can almost succeed in not letting it bother me, almost . . . except, even though I am trying hard not to be, I am still shaken by the dramatic change in the way Special Ed is treating me.

You knew the kid was crazy, I remind myself. *You knew that.*

"Okay . . . yeah . . . so, here's one of Dee Dee and Johnny. And see that car behind them? That belonged to Rod Stewart's manager," Special Ed explains the next picture, and I decide that since everyone is acting as if I don't exist anyway, I won't be intruding if I just stand behind them and look, because, actually, I, unlike say, Madeline, am really interested. This time Special Ed has rightly identified the two Ramones who are standing outside of CBGB's drinking bottles of beer, facing each other, though under their low, straight curtain of heavy bangs, their eyes are looking somehow beyond each other and at someone maybe approaching or maybe walking away. The car (some kind of shit Toyota) belonging to Rod Stewart's manager seems kind of suspect, but I call upon my hard-earned maturity and self-restraint and say nothing.

"And then this is Tom Verlaine, you know of Television . . . *Marquee Moon*, you know," Special Ed says of the next picture, which shows a guy in a ripped-to-shreds T-shirt passed out among the garbage cans, his exceptionally long arms splayed weirdly out to his sides as if he were falling through air from a great, great height.

"No, that's Richard Hell," I blurt out, having obviously used up all of my maturity and restraint, and once again, my correction is not appreciated as Special Ed and Madeline look back at me, Madeline with her usual blankness, but Eddie's big blue (yes, I have decided they are definitely blue) eyes conveying silent but palpable scorn.

"I'm sorry . . ." I say, realizing with a start that I actually like having this boy's eyes upon me and that what I really want is to have his attention again as I did that first day when the shift we worked together had been like running a marathon, trying to catch up with all that he had left undone, but fun, really fun, and I had to ask myself, *when was the last time I had fun with anyone?*

"No . . . I'm serious, that's Richard Hell," I say, and reach out and abruptly grab the stack of photos from his hands, pointing with an authority I have when it comes to very few things. "I mean, look at his nose. Look at the size of that head. Look at his *lips*, for God's sake. That's Hell."

A customer walks into the store and up to the beans-by-the-pound counter, and, with what I think I recognize as a sigh of relief, Madeline glides over to serve him.

"What's your problem?" Special Ed demands under his breath, and I watch with a disturbing amount of delighted fascination as his expression darkens. "I thought you were cool . . . but, like, wow! You totally fucked me up, man . . ."

"You mean with Madeline? Listen to me. You weren't doing too well before I butted in, and yes, I agree she's pretty, but really, don't you think she's kind of, well, dull?"

"Dull is in the eyes of the beholder, dude . . ." Special Ed continues to sulk and his lips get so adorably pouty that I do start to feel a little bit sorry for him. I mean, I knew from the start the kid wasn't right, that he was a little crazy, and what everyone knows about craziness is that it is not to be relied upon, and I guess that is what makes it so attractive to certain people such as myself and, I fear, Teddy. We like being left guessing. We like not knowing exactly where a person is coming from because they don't know, themselves. We, to our own peril, find instability alluring. But I was lucky. I dodged the bullet by marrying a steady man. (And with a shiver of fear, I wonder if Teddy will have the same luck visited upon her?) But where was that steady man? And why wasn't I with him instead of standing here trying way too hard to reclaim some sort of connection with a crazy person young enough to be my son?

"Do you want me to show you what Tom Verlaine looks like?" I ask gently, trying to find a way to make it up to this boy, because I know I should be above what I am clearly not.

"How 'bout this?" he asks, before roughly grabbing the

pictures from my hands and pointedly heading for the back-room. "How 'bout I just believe you on this one."

MY HUSBAND comes home for a surprise visit and it is as if I am pulled back with a giant hook through time. From the second he walks through the front door, I am suddenly the same person I was three months before, less myself and more like him but comfortable in this permutation, more comfortable than I am without him being a big part of me.

"I missed you," Phil says, taking me into his arms, his leather jacket smelling strongly of tobacco, even though Phil does not smoke.

"Yes," I say, because I know exactly what he means and hold him even tighter.

Together, we act like the old couple we are, speaking in unfinished sentences, referring to long, complicated stories with just a few key words, rising at dawn to walk the dog for two miles, drinking our coffee in matching cups covered with pictures of blueberries, going to the farmers' market and dividing the number of bags we carry home equally.

What we don't do is talk about Teddy. It is a subject we try studiously to avoid, but even so, her silent, invisible presence hangs over us like a too-densely woven blanket, keeping us close but also darkening our world.

"She didn't want to do it," Phil whispers into my head the last night of his visit, and I am grateful to be lying down finally because I have felt light-headed all day. I have been dizzy with the fear of losing him, really losing him, because I know I am at a dangerous moment in my life, where I have put in jeopardy everything I have that matters to me. But still, even knowing this, even fearing this, even after feeling dizzy all day at the thought of what tomorrow will be like without him, I do not feel ready to move.

"But she did do it," I say, and catch the sob that always seems to be standing in the wings, waiting to step up and take center stage at the first mention of what Teddy did.

"It was a mistake." Phil's voice is quiet and uncharacteristically sad. "She made a mistake. And now . . . you have to forgive her, Penny."

I don't know what to say because I think that is what I am trying to do, forgive Teddy for something that I can't seem to forgive her for. I know this is why she does not want to talk to me anymore. I know this is why she calls her father and rarely returns my calls. I know this is why she has gone skiing during her father's visit—not to avoid him, but because she so very much does not want to see *me*.

But what is it I cannot forgive her for? It isn't for what she tried to do to herself. I forgive her that. Of course, I forgive her that. So what is it? Did those crazy slashes across her wrists sever some notion I had falsely harbored of being in control? Was it the illusion—perhaps the one clung to by most mothers, who feel we must assume the role of benevolent fascist in the family to make our children feel protected—that spilled down the drain of Teddy's dorm bathroom sink? Is it my own lack of control, over everything, revealed by her act, which I can't forgive her for? Or do I just resent her for taking away *the illusion* that I ever had such control?

Phil holds me tighter and I notice the heat of our bodies

touching one another has caused us both to start to sweat, making the embrace feel tentative at best and nearly painful in its slickness and lack of certainty.

I GO into the backroom near the end of my shift to get some more half-pound bags and am not really surprised to see June Atkinson in there, doing inventory.

"Oh, hi, June," I say, opening the drawer in which the paper goods are stored. "How's it coming?"

"What, dear?"

"The inventory?"

"Oh . . . fine, dear," she says, and smiles sweetly and then goes back to her work, but when I glance over I notice the inventory sheet is just a plain piece of white paper on which she is busy drawing row after row of neatly rendered daisy heads.

"June?" I start to ask about the daisies, but decide not to. She, in her state of mock concentration, actually looks happy. She looks contented standing in this tiny room, doodling away her time, and who am I to disturb her?

I get the half-pound bags out of the drawer, but I don't feel like leaving right away.

"You know, I've never asked you this before, June, but do you have any children?" I say, really just stalling for time, and continue to watch, fascinated, as she draws two more identical daisies with exactly the same number of pedals.

"Four. Two boys and two girls and seven grandchildren." She, as always, answers my question in her friendly way, but gives me nothing more.

"And do they live near you?" I ask, getting a perverse amount of enjoyment watching this old woman pretending to do a serious job—a glimpse of myself in the future, perhaps? But what job will I be pretending to do then, I wonder? Who and what will I be trying to be that I am not really?

"Two live near. Two far away," she says with no emotion, no pain at the thought that some of her children are far from her and no delight that some are still close. Thinking about her children appears to bring forth nothing within her, which is strange. Believe me, for a mother, it is really strange. I watch as she draws a fast flower that appears to displease her. She frowns and erases harshly.

"Well . . . do you want to know about me?" I say, suddenly wanting to see if I can talk about Teddy in the same flat, emotionless way.

"What, dear?" June says before she more carefully redoes the bad daisy.

"About my daughter. You know, I do have a daughter . . ." I listen hard to see if I'm sounding neutral enough, but it is hard to tell.

"Oh. Yes?"

"Well," I falter, suddenly no longer interested in pursuing this conversation because I realize I don't know what to say. This is what it has come to. I no longer have words to describe my own child, the prime focus of what had been the prime of my life. But I must try to do this, I tell myself. I must learn to speak of her and do it with complete indifference.

"Well," I start again, and feel the vocal chords in my neck strain with the effort of trying to sound normal. "She's nineteen now, but when she was little . . . when Teddy was little, well, always, she worried about things. She was just a terrible worrier. Like, before she started to eat breakfast, she would need to know what the next meal of the day was going to be, and when we would go to the park she would immediately start to worry about when we were going to leave, and when we went swimming she would fret about how cold she would be when she got out of the pool and . . . and it was maddening to have a child like that. It drove me nuts! And I was always telling her, 'Teddy, be free! Be free, Teddy!'"

I stop because even I can hear the emotion in my voice. I can hear the sadness and fear and anger and regret and loss. I hear only what I do not want to hear and so I stop, but June just sighs in a contented way and pushes a lock of hair out of her face and continues her drawing.

"'Be free, Teddy,'" she repeats my last words in an oddly wistful way. "That's sweet."

I CALL my husband and tell him I am coming.

To MY shocked amazement, Manager Laurel is crushed when I give her my notice.

"But, you're my best worker!" she, the queen of no emotions, the one who floats above it all, whines childishly. "You can't do this to me!"

I say nothing, because we both know I can.

Now that I am leaving I ice-skate through my shifts, making little or no eye contact with anyone, keeping my thoughts to myself, thoughts that center almost entirely on all the things that must be done before I leave the country. During my breaks I study my language books and try to learn the lay of the land of what will be my new home by tracing my finger around maps and memorizing the names of streets and plazas and parks. None of it seems real to me and I wonder if it ever will. Occasionally, I go into the backroom and check my cell to see if Teddy has called. She hasn't, but maybe she will actually want to talk to me again when I am so far away from her. Maybe distance will make her love me again.

On my second-to-last day of work, I go out the back door of the Old Bean to dump a load of spent grounds and am suddenly grabbed from behind. I have that life-flashing-in-front-of-your-eyes moment where I think this is it, the knife, bullet, blunt object that is going to end it all and I hate the idea of it happening here in the smelly alley amongst all of the castoffs and odorous debris, but just as I brace myself for what I do not and cannot know, the grip loosens and a person presents himself, a person that I immediately recognize.

"You have to help me," Special Ed says with real urgency, and he does something with his bad mouth that is supposed to approximate a smile, I think, but his bright eyes do nothing but plead.

"How?" I say and place my hand over my thumping, thumping heart, grateful for the second chance when I thought all my chances were over.

"Dance with me."

"What?"

"I don't know, man. Everything's very confusing at the moment. Very confusing, and I think if I just do a dance. Like an old-fashioned one, you know, like a rhumba or mambo . . . the kind where there's like a right way to do it, I'll be, you know . . . fine, see? But the problem is I don't know how to do that kind of dance and so you are going to have to teach me."

Special Ed is speaking fast, and I think, *the kid is on speed, which is really not good.*

"Why do you think I know how to do that kind of dance?"

"Don't you? I mean . . . you're like the only person I know who might because everyone else I know definitely doesn't."

"Well, sorry, but I'm with them. I'm in with the definitely-doesn't crowd on this one."

"Oh shit!" Special Ed stamps his foot like a frustrated child and then runs his hands through his black spiky hair. For a brief second, I wonder if I would have found him adorable or disagreeable as a little kid. I wonder if he and Teddy would have played well. But then I realize I don't like thinking of him with Teddy, even as small children, and push the thought away. "Well, come on, Penny! Can't you just show me how to, well, you know, fake it a little?"

Faking it a little seems like something I may be able to show someone, but still, I look doubtfully around the alley that is so dismally gray and sticky smelling in the late afternoon shadows and ask, "Here?"

"Well . . . yeah. I mean, where else?"

I look at him for a few seconds. Outside he looks so pale and sickly, like someone who ingests all of the wrong things and none of the right ones. Why did I ever find boys like that attractive? What was it that made me want to lick their cool, stale-tasting, white skin? Was it their avant-gardedness? Was it their rebel stance? But there is nothing avant-garde about the way this boy looks now. He is an anachronism. A time-warp baby. He is really so very wrong.

"You know something, Special Ed? You're a mess," I say with both sadness and longing.

"Oh . . . come on, Penny. Can't you show me like, a fox-trot? Or how 'bout a cha-cha-cha? How hard could it be to like fake a fucking cha-cha-cha?"

"I'm leaving," I tell the boy. "I'm moving to the other side of the world, Special Ed."

"Right this fucking minute?"

"No, but soon," I say, and have to stop myself from crying because, really, when you get down to it, I don't like leaving anything or anywhere or anyone, really, even this mess of a boy who at this moment has decided to present himself to me like the winning question in a big contest. I know I could answer it correctly if I wanted to.

"Well, hey, Penny, time is short and life is long or maybe it goes the other way, but let's like, just *tango*, okay?" he says, and abruptly grabs my hand and pulls me close. He lays his cheek next to mine, and my nose fills with his sweet, licorice, and vaguely ether scent. I feel the pressure of his rock-formation teeth pressing against my jaw and imagine my own mouth collapsing, an absurd idea that seems almost probable just as he grips me tighter and rolls his head slightly so his lips suddenly capture mine, and how does it happen? How does the feel of someone's mouth against yours, even someone's horrible, too-young and crazy and confused mouth, how does the feel of those lips meeting yours make all that you have kept inside of you, your fears, disappointments, and perpetual uncertainties fly out into the shadows of the surrounding buildings, joining all those fumes rising from the fullest dumpster that overflows with crushed paper cups and last week's beans and cartons of souring milk, released by a kiss, set for only a second, but, oh, what a second, finally free?

ACKNOWLEDGMENTS

First and foremost I must thank Andrew Tonkovich, who is the reason that this book ever got published. Immeasurable thanks to Jim Krusoe, the best writer in America and also the best teacher. Special, special thanks to Monona Wali, a great writer, a great friend, and a great companion on this long, long trip. Thank you to my agent, Ethan Bassoff, and editor, Anne Horowitz; how lucky I am to get to work with such smart, lovely, and insightful people. And thanks to my dear friends for all of their help, support, advice, careful reading, and, well, friendship: Elinor Levine, Sam Maser, Tom Perrotta, David Shields, Dinah Lenney, Zoe Carter Fitzgerald, Charlie Fink, Joy Every, and Dylan Landis.